A FRENCH MASQUERADE

Barbara Chesney recklessly escapes an arranged marriage and is thankful to be offered the post of lady's maid to a young émigrée who has escaped from the turbulence of the French Revolution. When Barbara and her mistress are kidnapped, it is Barbara's quick thinking that enables her to change places with her mistress, never dreaming that she would be smuggled across the channel to face a revolutionary court in Paris. How will she be rescued when no-one knows she is there?

Books by Karen Abbott
in the Linford Romance Library:

RED ROSE GIRL
SUMMER ISLAND
A TIME TO FORGIVE
LOVE IS BLIND
LOVE CONQUERS ALL
A MATTER OF TRUST
DESIGNS FOR LOVE
WHEN TRUE LOVE WINS
A TASTE OF HAPPINESS
THE HEART KNOWS NO BOUNDS
THE TURNING TIDE
OUTRAGEOUS DECEPTION
RISING TO THE CALL

KAREN ABBOTT

---✦---

A FRENCH
MASQUERADE

Complete and Unabridged

LINFORD
Leicester

First published in Great Britain in 2004

First Linford Edition
published 2005

British Library CIP Data

Abbott, Karen
   A French masquerade.—Large print ed.—
Linford romance library
   1. Love stories
   2. Large type books
   I. Title
   823.9'14 [F]

   ISBN 1–84395–816–3

Published by
F. A. Thorpe (Publishing)
Anstey, Leicestershire

Set by Words & Graphics Ltd.
Anstey, Leicestershire
Printed and bound in Great Britain by
T. J. International Ltd., Padstow, Cornwall

This book is printed on acid-free paper

1

Agatha Marchant, seated primly on a straight-backed chair in her darkly-panelled parlour, smiled thinly at her niece, pleased to have been the one to let her know that her future was uncertain no longer.

A bright shaft of the early afternoon sunlight shimmered through the mullioned windows and lighted on the faded carpet. The rest of the room seemed dim in comparison. Dim and dismal.

For once, Barbara Chesney, seated at the opposite side of the unlit fireplace, didn't notice the drabness of the room. At that moment, her emotions matched its cheerless atmosphere. Her face had stiffened with shock and abhorrence as she heard her aunt's words, her fingers flying to cover her mouth. Now, she straightened her upper body and lifted her head.

'I'm sorry, Aunt Agatha! I cannot possibly agree to it! I would far rather go . . . go . . . go into a nunnery!' And she would, too. Anything would be better than marrying the odious Squire Bailey!

Mistress Marchant drew herself tightly upright and regarded her niece severely. 'Nonsense, Barbara! It is an extremely good offer . . . and you should be grateful to your Uncle Walter for having taken so much time and effort into getting Squire Bailey to offer for you. It wasn't easy, you know!'

Barbara actually laughed at that, though, in truth, her heart felt far from joyous. 'Then he won't be too upset to hear of my refusal, will he?'

'You seem to forget yourself, Barbara! As the orphaned daughter of a penniless vicar whose stipend barely kept you and Walter's dear sister, Lydia, in food and clothing, you have little to commend you!' She drew out a lace-edged handkerchief and dabbed her eyes. 'Poor Lydia! If she were alive today she would weep with gratitude to see you exalted thus!'

'My dear Mamma would weep to see me married to a man old enough to be my grandfather!' Barbara replied with spirit, rising to her feet.

'Then you must bear the consequences, you ungrateful girl!' Agatha also rose to her feet. Although her niece was by no means small, Agatha towered over her, the ostrich feathers in her satin turban quivering on the top of her severely drawn-back hair. 'Mr Marchant will support you no longer! We have our dear Amaryllis to think of. A London Season is extremely expensive, you know!'

'Then maybe Amaryllis should marry Squire Bailey, if he is such a good catch!' Barbara said boldly. 'For I assure you, I will not!'

Aunt Agatha's eyes gleamed through narrowed slits as she drew back her head. 'How dare you speak to me in this fashion! You had better retire to

3

your room . . . and remain there until tomorrow!'

As she spoke, the hauteur of her expression crumpled. 'Oh, dear! Have you no sensibility, Barbara? I don't know what Mr Marchant will say when he returns home tonight! Oh, dear!'

At her aunt's distress, Barbara was immediately contrite. She reached forward and touched her aunt's arm. 'I really am sorry, Aunt Agatha. I am truly grateful that you and Uncle Walter have cared for me since Mamma and Papa died of the fever when I was small. But what you ask of me now is awful. Dear Aunt, please try to understand! When I marry . . . if I marry . . . I would wish to marry for love as my parents did.'

Agatha's expression softened slightly. 'I fear you are too fanciful, Barbara. Your mamma and papa did indeed marry for love . . . but it didn't keep them warm in wintertime! Nor did it protect them from the fever. Thomas Chesney has much to answer for, taking dear Lydia into the slums of London like that.'

'Papa did what he thought best. He was called of God to serve the poor!' Barbara hotly defended her beloved father.

'That's as maybe . . . but he left you without a penny to your name. You will be twenty years of age in a month's time. Are you to don a spinsters' cap and spend the rest of your days in menial service?'

Barbara tilted her head high. 'If need be, I have no objection to earning my living. I am perfectly sure that God, whom my father loved and trusted, will keep me under his wing. He will not desert me.'

Barbara was thankful to escape upstairs to her room. Her cousin, Amaryllis, was awaiting her, her face pink with expectancy.

'Did Mamma tell you, Babs? Were you surprised? What did you say?' The questions babbled out of Amaryllis's mouth. She was younger than Barbara by three years and, in Barbara's opinion, more than a little spoiled by her doting parents.

Barbara looked at her coolly. 'You know what your mama wished to say to me?'

Amaryllis tossed back her dark hair. 'Of course! I think it a wonderful idea! You'll be mistress of Bailey House! You'll probably have your own pony and trap and a whole wardrobe of lovely dresses! I almost envy you, Babs!'

'Then your envy is unfounded, Lissa, for I have no intention of accepting Squire Bailey's offer. Did you seriously consider that I would? He is so old. And ugly!'

'Pah! What matters all of that? As you say, he is old . . . he will die soon and then you'll be rich.'

Barbara was shocked. 'Lissa! How can you say such things? I know I have said I cannot marry him — but I don't wish him dead.'

Amaryllis shrugged her delicate shoulders, her lips pouting. 'Then, what will you do? I overheard Papa saying that you would have to obey him, that he will keep you locked in your room until you agree to the marriage . . . or else he would wash his hands of you!'

Barbara stared at her. 'You mean I will have to leave? That I cannot stay here in some serving capacity?'

'That's what he said! Mind you, I'm sure I could twist him around and ask for you to become my maid. It's high time I had one. Wh . . . what are you doing?' She stopped and looked at Barbara in astonishment.

'What does it look like? I am collecting my things together.'

'But . . . why?'

'Because, Lissa, it seems I have no alternative. If Uncle Walter is so determined to make me marry that loathsome man, then I must flee before he returns home, for, once he is here, he may prevent me going.'

'But . . . where will you go? What will you do?'

Barbara's shoulders sagged briefly. 'I

don't know.' Suddenly her eyes brightened. 'I have an idea! . . . No, I mustn't tell you . . . Uncle Walter might make you divulge it. Please don't ask, Lissa!' She took Amaryllis's hands in her own. 'But you will help me, won't you? Give me the opportunity to get away?'

Amaryllis stepped back a little. 'I . . . I'm not sure. Papa will be most upset. Oh, I beg of you, don't go!'

'I must, Lissa.'

'But you've no money. And so few possessions!'

'I'll manage. I'll find some employment. It surely won't be all that difficult. I can write a neat hand and draw passably. I'll be a governess or some such. Really, Lissa, there is no need to worry about me!'

Amaryllis tugged her ruby ring off her finger. 'Then, at least accept this, Babs. You will be able to sell it and live off the proceeds for a while.'

Barbara was loathe to do so, but, at her cousin's insistance, took it in her hand. 'Thank you, dear cousin. I will

8

only sell it if I absolutely have to. Now, go down to your mamma and make sure she remains in the parlour for the next half hour.' She hugged Amaryllis tightly. They hadn't always got on well together but she was grateful for her cousin's generosity and compliance in this moment of need.

She waited for a few moments, giving Amaryllis time to reach the parlour and engage her mother in conversation. She then wrapped her cloak around her shoulders, picked up her portmanteau and slipped quietly out of her room, down the back stairs and out through the side door.

Her destination was the vicarage and her friend, Violet, the minister's daughter.

Violet's initial joy at seeing her friend turned into dismay as Barbara unfolded her tale.

'You must stay here, Barbara! I'm sure Papa will know what to do. Unfortunately, he has been called away to see a parishioner who is dying. He will be home by morning, if not before.' Her face sobered. 'He may feel it is your duty to obey your uncle . . . but I am sure he will not see you forced into marriage against your wishes.'

'I cannot take that risk. I think I need to get further away, Violet. I had thoughts of . . . ' She smiled self-consciously. 'You know how my parents felt called by the Lord to go to London to help the poor people in those dreadful slums? I have the fancy to go there also.'

Violet looked horrified. 'Not in the slums, Babs! How would you survive? Your parents had each other . . . and the bishop's sanction of Reverend Chesney's living. But you . . . you have been genteelly reared . . . and are a single woman. You would be most vulnerable!'

Barbara shook her head. 'No, nothing so radical! I have thoughts more along the lines of becoming a governess or a companion to a lady.'

A look of incredulity lit Violet's face.

'How strange! A friend of dear Mamma's is in the parlour at this very moment. She was just telling me such a strange tale and knows someone in London with that very need. She has just returned from visiting the lady in question and called in here on her way back to Cheshire, where she now lives.'

Lady Templeton was indeed pleased to see Barbara. She looked at her closely through her lorgnette, clearly liking what she saw. 'Tell me all about yourself, Miss Chesney,' she invited.

Barbara told Lady Templeton all that she knew about herself and her parents . . . and about her uncle and aunt's care of her over the past twelve years . . . and their present determination to coerce her into marrying the elderly squire.

Lady Templeton turned her gaze onto Violet. 'And you, my dear? You will confirm Miss Chesney's tale . . . and vouch for her good character?' She turned apologetically towards Barbara. 'Forgive me, my dear, but I have to be sure before I can recommend you.'

Violet answered at once. 'Oh, yes! We have been friends for these past twelve years, ever since Babs arrived here. Papa also would have no hesitation in giving his blessing. Perhaps if you could stay until he arrives home, Lady Templeton, he will tell you so himself.'

'I regret I cannot do that,' Lady Templeton said slowly. 'I must be on my way within the hour. However . . . what do you say if I were to write a letter of recommendation to Lady Birchley, telling her of your good character and beseeching her to take you on trial?'

Barbara had no doubts whatsoever. 'Oh, yes, please, Lady Templeton!' She paused, and then asked, 'What exactly is the position you have in mind for me, Lady Templeton?'

'I think the general term would be to describe your task as companion to Lady Birchley's new 'ward'. More than that, I cannot say.' She leaned forward. 'You may think all of this to be highly unorthodox . . . but, then, so is Lady Birchley's position in this matter. I must ask for your fullest discretion. Not a word to anyone. You agree?'

Barbara nodded, an excited gleam in her eyes.

'Now, before I go,' Lady Templeton said, pulling open the string of her reticule. 'Here is enough money to get you to Lady Birchley's home . . . and here is her address.'

Once Lady Templeton and her maid had departed, Barbara grasped hold of Violet's hands and danced in glee. 'Oh, it couldn't be better, Violet! I must be off at once!'

Violet laughed at her friend's enthusiasm. 'The last stage has long gone, Barbara. You must stay until morning. The ten o'clock stage will be early enough for you to reach London before nightfall. Now, what shall I tell your uncle? He is bound to suspect you called here.'

Barbara's smile slipped away. 'I fear so. He will hate having to lose face to

Squire Bailey . . . but I have no alternative!'

Barbara tucked the piece of paper into her pocket and patted it happily. 'I fear Uncle Walter might set out after me and try to force me to return, so it's best that you don't know where I am going, Violet. I don't want you to have to tell lies about it. When I am settled in, I will write to let you know. I am sure Lady Birchley will frank a letter for me. I will also write to my uncle. In fact, I will write to him now and then all you need to do is to give him my letter when he calls.'

As the first streaks of daylight lightened the sky, a rapid banging on the outside rear door underneath her window made her leap out of bed.

It wasn't her uncle. It was a young boy. Why, it was Alfie, their boot boy! Whatever was he doing here at this hour?

'Alfie? What is it? What do you want?'

'They knows you're here, Miss Barbara! I heard 'em shouting! Miss

14

Amaryllis said this was likely where you'd be. They're bringing the carriage to take you back.'

Barbara's heart seemed to have stopped beating for a moment. She wouldn't go back! She couldn't! She realised Violet had joined them and turned anxiously to her.

'I must leave at once, Violet, before it is too late. Please explain to your father, Violet. I would rather have seen him before I go, but I daren't risk waiting for his return.'

The two girls ran down the stairs and back to the kitchen, where Alfie was waiting.

'What you going to do, Miss Barbara? Are you running away? The master weren't half mad.'

'Yes, Alfie. I am running away . . . but you mustn't tell anyone that you have seen me.'

'That's all right, Miss Barbara. I want to come with you.'

'Oh! I'm not sure . . . '

'You gotta let me. Miss Amaryllis

don't like me. She pinches and nips me.'

Barbara looked sympathetically at him. 'I'm not absolutely sure what I'll be doing myself yet, Alfie. Lady Birchley may not want me and life in the city can be very hard.'

'I'll do anything, Miss Barbara. Just give me a chance. I can help to carry your luggage. Anything.'

Barbara considered this. 'All right, Alfie! You may come with me but we must leave at once.'

The stagecoach arrived on time; the two passengers boarded it and it swiftly sped on its way. It wasn't a comfortable journey. Alfie was seated outside beside the driver, but Barbara was squashed between an extremely fat lady who was balancing an equally fat baby on her short lap and a shabbily-dressed man whose body odour was none too pleasant.

Just before noon, the coach slowed down and rumbled into the cobbled yard of the Silver Angel where they

16

were to stop for some refreshments. Barbara followed the plump lady to the room laid aside for the female passengers, telling Alfie to remain close by. After assisting her female companion into a comfortable seat, she found her way to the kitchen to order some food.

When it was time to pay for their refreshments, she was horrified to discover that her reticule was missing. Ashen-faced, she hurried outside and bade Alfie search the floor of the stagecoach but with no success.

Their money had gone.

2

'You've been robbed, dearie!' the plump lady declared. 'I always keep my money close to my body.' She delved down the front of her bodice and pulled out a small purse. 'But, never mind. I'll settle your bill with mine.'

When they resumed their journey, unsurprisingly, the shabbily-dressed man was no longer with them.

'You mark my words. It was him,' the fat lady declared. 'Don't trust nobody when you're travelling, dearie. Don't trust nobody.'

Barbara was sorry to bid her farewell at the next staging-post and was too proud to ask her for further assistance. The other passengers alighted one by one and when the coach arrived at its final destination in London only Barbara and Alfie remained. According to Lady Templeton's written instructions this was where they had to hire a hackney carriage for the last stage of their journey.

'What we gonna do, Miss Barbara?' Alfie wanted to know.

'Wait! There is Amaryllis's ring. Oh, no!' With dismay, she remembered it was in her reticule.

'Cor! You mean the one you pinched off her?' Alfie breathed in admiration.

Barbara gaped at him. 'Indeed not! She gave it to me, to help me!'

'That's not what she said to Mr Marchant, Miss Barbara. She said you'd pinched it!'

Barbara stared at him in horror. 'But, I didn't.' Her fingers spread across her parted lips. 'Do you mean Uncle Walter thinks I'm a thief?'

Alfie nodded.

'Oh, no! And now it's been stolen. Oh, Alfie, what are we to do?'

A smartly-driven carriage drawn by two dark stallions swept into the yard of the inn and a tall young man, wearing tightly-fitted fawn pantaloons, immaculately-shining black boots and a many-caped cloak sprang down from the driver's seat, tossing the reins to the young boy who leaped down from the step at the back of the carriage. As he passed in front of Barbara, he bowed politely and raised his hat revealing his dark, wavy hair, murmuring, 'Good-day to you, ma'am.'

Although his glance had only momentarily swept over her, Barbara felt an intense frisson of excitement flow through her body, banishing all concerns about being thought a thief. The man continued on his way into the inn and Barbara stared after him, the memory of his handsome face and the intensity of his dark grey eyes imprinted on her mind.

He was obviously a man about town; a 'Corinthian' even, she wondered, having read the term in a penny broadsheet; a 'Nonpareil'. With a heartfelt sigh, she glanced down at the skirt of her serviceable gown and faded woollen cloak. She had never felt poorly dressed in the village where she had grown up but now, having seen the clothes the young man was wearing, she felt positively dowdy.

She mentally shook herself. Day-dreaming about an unknown, handsome young man was not going to get her to Lady Birchley's residence. And where had Alfie got to?

'Alfie?'

Suddenly, he was back at her side. He took hold of her hand and began to pull her towards the waiting carriage. 'Quick, Miss Barbara. Get into the luggage box on the back of the carriage. I'll take care of the lad.'

'But, Alfie, why? How will that help us to get to Lady Birchley's?'

'I heard him talk about her. He's going there.'

'Who?'

'Him! The flash dandy!'

Alfie ran over to where the lad was standing, feeding some bags of oats to the two horses. Barbara looked around uncertainly, by no means convinced of the wisdom of Alfie's plan. But, what else were they to do?

With no more ado, she lifted the hem of her skirt and scrambled up onto the back of the carriage. Fortunately the box was unlocked and, with no further hesitation, she clambered inside. The lid dropped down on top of her, shutting out the light. Her heart was racing. What was she doing here, behaving in this uncharacteristic way?

She almost changed her mind and made a move to lift the lid. Before she could do so, light flooded the box and Alfie hastily scrambled in.

'Sorry, Miss,' he apologised as he landed on top of her.

They had little time to rearrange themselves. Barbara was aware of the carriage bouncing, presumably as its driver climbed back aboard, and it immediately jerked into movement, rattling uncomfortably over the cobbled yard.

Alfie was flung against her as the carriage swung in a tight circle.

They came to an abrupt stop.

Before Alfie had time to extricate himself from his position, the lid of the box was flung wide open and a harsh male voice commanded. 'Out!'

Barbara grimaced wryly into Alfie's eyes, no more than two inches above her own. 'Best do as he says, Alfie.'

As Alfie raised himself and vaulted over the top edge, Barbara sat up gingerly.

'And what do you think you were up to, my lad?' the man was demanding of Alfie as she peeped over the top of the box. As expected, it was the handsome young man from the inn.

'Don't you dare hit him!' Barbara cried in alarm.

The man raised his eyes and betrayed utter amazement at her presence. 'Another urchin stowaway, I declare!' A bemused grin split across his face as he straightened his body, placing his rounded fists on his hips.

Barbara indignantly rose to her feet and faced him squarely, her own hands

23

in similar position. 'Indeed, sir, I am no urchin! And, I must add, you drive your carriage in an extremely wild and reckless manner.'

'Indeed?' His lips made a lop-sided smile and the corners of his eyes crinkled into fine lines as he coolly regarded her. 'Were you an invited guest in my carriage, I would have driven more carefully.'

Barbara hesitated, momentarily thrown by his amused scrutiny. 'Yes, well, I must apologise for . . . for . . . our action, sir.' Barbara took a deep breath and held her chin high. 'I am sorry to have stolen a ride in your carriage, sir. It was most unwise of us . . . but we were . . . desperate. Quite desperate.'

'Ah! That explains it, then. And what was the cause of your desperation? I must admit, I find it difficult to imagine what cause would compel a young lady to conceal herself so uncomfortably in my luggage box.'

Barbara weighed up the man's character and decided that she could trust him with the truth of her predicament without him taking undue advantage of her. 'We were robbed of all our money, sir. We could think of no other way to proceed on our journey.'

The man's eyebrows rose. 'And why choose my carriage? I could be heading anywhere.'

'I heard you, mister. You're going to see Lady Birchley!' Alfie interrupted again.

'Boy! Go and talk to my livery boy!' the man growled, pointing to where the young lad was holding the horses' reins. He turned back to Barbara, who towered above him from her stance in the luggage box. 'So?'

'Like Alfie said, he overheard you say that you were intending to visit Lady Birchley . . . and that is where we are going . . . to take up a position there.'

'And what position would that be?'

'To be a lady's maid, sir . . . or a companion. I am not sure which,' she confessed.

'You have proof of this?'

'Yes. I mean, no. That is, the letter was stolen, you see, along with our money.' Her face fell and her arms dropped to her sides. 'And I don't know how to get in touch with Lady Templeton again . . . not immediately, anyway.'

'You know Lady Templeton?'

'Yes . . . though only briefly. I met her at a friend's house yesterday. She thought me suitable for a position in Lady Birchley's household. She wrote a letter for me to give to Lady Birchley but it was in my reticule that was stolen from me.'

The man regarded her thoughtfully. 'You could return home and get in touch with Lady Templeton again.'

'No! No, I cannot! That would never do!'

The man's eyebrows rose again. 'Your parents aren't in favour of your present course of action?'

'My parents are long dead, sir. My aunt and uncle have cared for me these past twelve years. Only . . . ' she

26

grimaced. Oh, what was there to lose? 'My uncle was insisting that I marry an odious old man and I refused!' She thrust out her chin defiantly.

'That is indeed a desperate enough cause,' he agreed solemnly. He held out his hand. 'Come! I think I believe your tale. Take my hand and I will help you down.'

Barbara took hold of his extended hand, wondering if he was aware of the tremors that ran through her arm, and stepped over the edge of the box onto the step. The man released her hand and took hold of her around her slim waist and easily swung her down to the ground.

Breathlessly, Barbara looked up at him, her heart beating a ragged pattern. His smile set a tingle rippling through her body and his eyes seemed to look upon her kindly. She felt assured that he would deal with her compassionately. 'What am I to do, sir?'

His words confirmed her thoughts. 'I will take you to Lady Birchley's home and she will decide what to do with you.'

'And Alfie?'

'Aye, and the lad, since he has been brave enough to try to protect you. Come! Up you get.'

On arrival at Carlton House, Lady Birchley's London residence, Barbara was ushered into a small parlour and Alfie was sent down to the kitchen.

Barbara glanced around. It was a pleasant room. The walls were covered in the palest of off-white paper decorated with narrow gold vertical stripes; the furniture was simple yet elegant; the floor was carpeted in green, giving a restful air; a tall vase of flowers adorned a small table set in the window-alcove.

She wandered over to the window and looked outside across the smooth grass of the lawn, bordered by wide flowerbeds bursting with colour on this early summer's day.

The sound of the door opening drew her swiftly around. A tall, elegant lady about the age of Barbara's aunt was approaching her. She was smiling pleasantly and Barbara instinctively dropped in a low curtsey.

'Come and sit over here,' the lady bade her, indicating two cushioned, straight-backed chairs placed either side of a spindle-legged table.

Barbara carefully seated herself, suddenly thankful of her aunt's insistence that both she and Amaryllis deported themselves correctly at all times.

'I am Lady Birchley,' the lady introduced herself. 'Tell me something about yourself, my dear. You are called Barbara, I believe?'

Barbara felt her cheeks redden. Her rescuer had noted her name, then! 'Yes, ma'am. Barbara Chesney. My father, the Reverend Thomas Chesney was a minister of the church here in London until both he and my mother died of the fever twelve years ago.'

Under close questioning, Barbara recounted as much as she knew about herself and her family, even about the ruby ring that Amaryllis had given to her and later accused her of stealing. She endeavoured to speak kindly of her aunt and uncle for the years they had cared for her, but, nonetheless, expressed her loathing of their choice of husband for her.

Lady Birchley nodded sympathetically. 'I, too, married for love,' she said softly, her eyes glazing slightly as she remembered her late-husband. 'Now, Lady Templeton is a dear friend of mine and, on her recommendation, which I shall verify by letter, of course,' Lady Birchley added with a smile, 'I am prepared to offer you the position of companion and lady's maid to my ward, a young woman who has recently come over here from France. Are you willing to become Catrine's personal maid, Barbara?'

Barbara clasped her hands together. Had she heard correctly? It sounded too good to be true. 'Oh, yes, Lady Birchley! I would love that!'

'It isn't an easy life, Barbara. You will

be at Catrine's beck and call at all hours of the day or night. None of the high-society life for you, I'm afraid. You will still be on the outside looking in . . . but it will be a ring-side seat,' she added with a smile.'

'Oh, I won't mind that, Lady Birchley. Oh, how can I ever thank you?'

'By doing a good job, Barbara. You must learn all you can from my maid, Annie . . . and Catrine will help you, of course. I will clothe you with day-gowns and undergarments . . . and you will sleep in the ante-room off Catrine's bedroom. But, you are under age . . . just,' she added quickly, seeing Barbara's face fall. 'I think I must pay a visit to your uncle, Barbara . . . No, don't be alarmed, you will remain here. I will tell him that I have taken you into my employment and that he need no longer feel responsible for your welfare. Have you any questions?'

Barbara felt herself to be in a whirl of excitement. It all seemed so perfect.

'No, I can't think of anything. Oh, yes . . . what will happen to Alfie? He came to warn me and I feel I owe him my thanks, at the very least.'

'I gave instructions for him to be billeted over the stable block. He seems a lively boy.' Her eyes danced with merriment.

Barbara joined in, nodding her head. 'He seems impressed already with . . . ' Barbara paused. 'I'm sorry. I don't know the name of the man who had brought us here.'

'That is Lord Maximillian Rockfort, Barbara. Lady Templeton's nephew.'

3

Annie, Lady Birchley's maid, took Barbara upstairs, where she was given a bowl of water for washing herself and two gowns to wear. One was pale blue and the other a shade of mauve. Barbara selected the mauve to wear today.

Annie then led her to Lady Birchley's sitting-room, where a slender young lady was seated on a sofa, listening eagerly to what Lady Birchley was saying. Barbara couldn't understand the words. It must be French, she decided, hoping she wouldn't be required to learn the language.

She couldn't help staring around the room. Its décor was in shades of cream and pale yellows, giving the impression that the sun was always shining.

Lady Birchley saw her hesitating at the door. 'Ah, Barbara! Come over here and meet Mademoiselle Catrine Azaire.'

Barbara smiled and curtsied slightly.

'I am pleased to meet with you,' Catrine said shyly. 'You will be my maid, oui? Lady Birchley is so kind!' She leaned towards her patron and gave a quick kiss on her cheek, then turned, hands out-stretched, to Barbara. She clasped both of Barbara's hands in her own tiny ones. 'I have longed for a friend, Barbara. I think you and I be good friends.'

Catrine's accent was charming. Her voice was low and musical. She was very pretty. Her dark brown hair was fashioned into ringlets gathered together and fastened high on her head. Barbara noticed that, although her eyes lit up when she spoke, a sadness lurked in her unguarded expression and she wondered what had caused it.

Over the next few days, Barbara gradually learned her duties as a lady's maid. The day was long, beginning before Catrine awakened and ending after Catrine had retired for the night. But the hours in between didn't seem like work ... it was as if she and Catrine were two friends enjoying each other's company. They giggled their way through applying make-up, brushing each other's hair, trying on gowns of silk and muslin and, apart from the more expensive cut and material of Catrine's day-gowns, they might both have been of equal standing.

Wanting to make sure Alfie was happy in his new position, Barbara was pleased when Catrine suggested that they walked out in the garden.

'I have not been out very much yet,' Catrine explained, when they were outside, 'because I am only lately come from France and there could be danger. I have not to talk about it, you understand. But I think I can tell you because you are my friend. They are calling it the Reign of Terror in my country. This last month or so, any person can accuse another of being an aristocrat and that person will be arrested. They will have a quick trial and then . . . ' She drew a finger under her chin. 'They have their head cut off! Madame Guillotine, they call it! It is terrible!'

Her pretty face was sad for a moment and two tiny tears appeared in the corners of her eyes. 'Two years ago my parents were denounced and they are dead,' she said flatly. Then she shrugged her shoulders. 'Every family has suffered. I am one of the lucky ones. Some brave men rescue me and bring me here. They say I must look forward and be happy . . . so I try my best. I only think of my parents when I am alone . . . then nobody see me cry.' She laid her hands over her heart. 'But sometimes I feel so sad here.'

Barbara impulsively hugged her. 'My parents are dead, too, so I understand.'

Their walk through the garden led towards the stables where they could see a couple of grooms exercising some horses and stable boys sweeping the soiled straw into a pile at one side of the yard.

Barbara spied a small figure seated on a three-legged stool, hunched over a leather saddle he was polishing. 'Alfie!' she called, stepping towards him.

The boy looked up and a delighted grin spread across his face. 'Miss Barbara! Cor! You looks a dandy! Are you a toff, now?'

Barbara and Catrine walked over to him. 'No . . . but Mademoiselle Catrine is. You must learn to bow to her, Alfie. Do you like it here?'

'Cor! Yes! And it ain't 'arf posh! I sleeps up there,' pointing above the stable, 'and I gets me grub wi' t'other lads in't tackle room. We landed on our feet 'ere, Miss Barbara, didn't we?'

Barbara smiled at his enthusiastic voice. 'We certainly did, Alfie. Thank you for being such a help to me.'

At the beginning of the following week, a hand-delivered note arrived. Catrine and Barbara were sitting in Lady Birchley's front parlour, both engrossed in embroidering some fine lawn handkerchiefs when Lady Birchley swept in.

'We are to have some visitors this afternoon,' she announced. 'Lord Rockfort and his cousin, Philip, wish to pay their respects to you, Catrine, dear. You must change your gown. I will come upstairs and help you to choose one . . . and, Barbara, you must wear the pale blue gown I gave you. It suits your colouring, I think.'

Her words caused quite a flutter and brought some pink colouring to the cheeks of both girls.

In the privacy of Catrine's boudoir, Catrine said excitedly. 'They are my favourite beaux. It is the third time they come. Lady Birchley says I shall have many more beaux, when I attend balls. I like having many beaux. Have you a beau, Barbara?'

'An admirer, do you mean? Then, no,' Barbara sighed. She smiled ruefully, pushing away the unbidden memory of Lord Rockfort's arms lifting her down from the back of his carriage.

It seemed like another lifetime away. Lord Rockfort had probably forgotten her already.

Catrine's eyes were dancing with mischief. 'I have a very good idea, Barbara. I will teach you some French words so that when we go to balls, and the young men will think you are French and fall in love with you! It is a good idea, oui? And you will be able to speak to me in my own language a little when I talk of being in love with my beaux, oui?'

Barbara laughed. 'I will try, Catrine.'

Under Lady Birchley's guidance, Catrine dressed in white sprigged muslin, with a wide dusky pink sash around her slim waist and some tiny pink flowers fixed into her hair.

Barbara already loved Catrine as though she were a sister — and the fact that they were both without any immediate family seemed to bond them together more closely. She could only wish her well in her promising love-match with Lord Rockfort, however much her own heart ached for her own cause.

It was the first time Barbara had worn the pale blue gown. It suited her colouring and accentuated her slim figure and taller stature than that of her mistress.

They seated themselves in the spacious drawing-room, a room so elegant it took Barbara's breath away every time she entered it. She chose a seat in a far corner, anxious to be as discreet as possible. Lady Birchley had already instructed her to address Lord Rockfort as 'm'lord' and his cousin as 'sir', if the occasion arose.

It was a relief when the two men were ushered into the room by the second footman. Both ladies stood to sink into low curtsies, whilst the two men made an elaborate bow. Barbara's own curtsey went unnoticed and she was glad to resume her discreet presence on the seat in the corner by an open window, from where she felt it safe to view their visitors without notice whilst she busied herself with some embroidery.

Lord Rockfort was elegantly dressed. His unpowdered hair gleamed as he bowed low. His dark green, cutaway coat revealed the lower edge of a striped green and gold waistcoat.

His eyes unexpectedly caught hers and she blushed as she quickly turned her gaze to her needlework, accidentally pricking her finger on her needle as she did so. Her slight jump brought a glimmer of a smile to his face before he returned his attention to the ladies.

Lord Rockfort's back was now towards Barbara and she raised her head slightly, enough to allow her to view Philip Grafton through her eyelashes without detection. From the light in his eyes as he conversed with Catrine, he seemed to be an unwitting rival to his older cousin for Catrine's affections.

He was paying very pretty compliments to Catrine, his young face alight as she coquettishly replied in her delightful French accent. Barbara noticed that her glance kept sliding back to Lord Rockfort, whose expression remained attentive as he listened to the young buck at his side talking animatedly about his hunting prowess and his description of himself as being a 'bruising rider'.

'I say, Maxie! Let's arrange a dash around the park, shall we?' Philip pleaded earnestly, oblivious to the cringing movement Lord Rockfort made at the shortened version of his name. He turned back to Catrine. 'It will be a grand lark, mademoiselle. Do say yes!'

He remembered his courtesy towards Lady Birchley and leapt to his feet to make a bow before her. 'That is, with your permission, Lady Birchley! Forgive me if I have acted impetuously. I can only plead that Mademoiselle Catrine's beauty blinds me to social niceties.' He beamed around, sure of his request being granted.

Lady Birchley exchanged a glance with Lord Rockfort. Barbara couldn't see his reaction but it must have been favourable because Lady Birchley gave her permission.

Catrine glanced coquettishly at her older beau. 'And, you also, Lord Rockfort? Will you join us on our dash around the park?' She smiled most beguilingly at him.

Lord Rockfort inclined his head. 'I am a trifle too old to wish to dash around the park, Mademoiselle Catrine . . . but I will promise to be sure I am riding that way at the time of your outing. Shall we say eleven o'clock on Wednesday forenoon? Good.'

He rose from his seat, motioning to his cousin to rise also, and bowed politely to both ladies.

Catrine sank gracefully into a low curtsey in front of him. 'Thank you, m'lord. You do me a great honour.' She smiled up into his face, looking so pretty that Barbara was sure she must steal his heart, if indeed it wasn't already in Catrine's possession.

Lord Rockfort raised her by the hand

and touched her fingers with his lips. 'I am pleased to find you so settled with Lady Birchley, Mademoiselle. Now, we must bid you good day. Come, Philip, take your leave of the ladies.' He made his bow to Lady Birchley, whilst Philip did likewise to Catrine.

During the next day and a half, Catrine didn't cease talking about the handsome Lord Rockfort and his cousin, Philip. 'La! I am not sure that I know which one I like the most!' she confided to Barbara, her eyes sparkling with the thrill of being courted by two beaux. 'Philip is a very nice boy . . . but Lord Rockfort is so handsome, is he not? And, being a lord, he has the greater appeal.' She sighed dramatically.

Wednesday dawned a beautiful day. Catrine eagerly bade Barbara to spread out her entire wardrobe of suitable attire for the carriage ride, holding first one gown and then another before her, viewing her reflection in the full-length looking-glass. She eventually chose the mid green, after Barbara had pronounced it ideal for the summer's day.

Every sound outside had Catrine running to peep through the front window, determined not to miss one second of their promised outing. Her vigil was at last rewarded and an equally excited Philip leapt down from his carriage, drawn by a pair of matching greys.

'Oh, la! He is as handsome as his cousin!' Catrine declared in rapture. She turned to grin delightedly to Barbara. 'I think, Barbara, that I like best which ever of my beaux is present with me at the time!'

The two young ladies flouted all society rules and were eagerly waiting in the front hall when Philip was admitted by the first footman.

'Mademoiselle Catrine!' Philip exclaimed, showing a very handsome leg in his extravagant bow.

Catrine dropped into a low curtsey, gazing up impishly into his eyes. 'Monsieur!' she murmured, lowering

45

her eyelashes coyly.

Barbara made a brief curtsey, not wanting to draw any attention to herself. The young man's eyes flickered over her briefly before Catrine was the centre of his attention once more.

Catrine remembered the social etiquette and drew Philip towards the parlour, where Lady Birchley was now waiting. Etiquette demanded a few moments of polite conversation, but at last Lady Birchley took pity on the young pair and rose from her chair to bid them on their way.

Philip ushered Catrine and her maid out of the house and down the wide curved steps that graced the front entrance. His top-hatted groom had already let down the step and was now standing by the horses' heads, restraining their impatience to be off.

Barbara caught sight of Alfie, dodging around the other side of the carriage, in danger of being caught by a flying hoof if he wasn't careful, she feared.

Philip leapt into the driving seat, his many capes flying out behind him. 'Let them go, Harry!' he called as he scooped up the reins with one hand and the long-handled whip with the other. The greys didn't need a second bidding. Their hooves dug into the gravel and the carriage took off.

Catrine squealed in delight as they took the corner of the drive on two wheels, her hand on her hat. 'Ooh, la la!'

The two ladies were almost hysterical by the time they turned through the park gates, where Philip had to slow his pace to accommodate other road users. Summer was sweeping on and the trees and flowers in the park were at their best, giving a glorious background of colour for the fine carriages as they swept along the winding tracks. They were bowling along at a cracking pace when the sound of hoof beats drummed behind them.

Barbara glanced over her shoulder, half-afraid that it might mean danger to

Catrine but she instantly recognised Lord Rockfort astride a magnificent black stallion, her heart leaping with admiration at the fine figure that he cut.

Philip hauled on the reins and the greys responded immediately. 'Good morning, Coz!' Philip called exuberantly. 'A fine day!'

'Good morning, Philip! Ladies!' Lord Rockfort doffed his hat, bowing gracefully from the waist.

'Lord Rockfort,' she murmured quietly.

Catrine greeted him with a wide smile. 'Lord Rockfort! Quel plaisir!' She rattled off some sentences in French.

By her gestures, Barbara gathered she was extolling Philip's prowess at the reins and was impressed when Lord Rockfort replied in the same language.

Lord Rockfort dismounted from his horse with one fluid movement as Philip tossed the reins to his livery boy and leapt down from the driving seat. 'How was that, Mademoiselle Catrine?'

he enquired, his face flushed with the thrill of the drive.

'Ah! C'est magnifique!' Catrine exclaimed. 'I would like to try it myself!'

'Any time!' Philip agreed with alacrity, his face betraying his imagined delight at the prospect of holding her slender hands upon the reins and sitting closely enough to that delectable body to enable him to control the horses.

'I will arrange some professional tuition, Mademoiselle,' Lord Rockfort assured her as he handed her down from the carriage. He was holding the reins of his horse loosely in his left hand. Unexpectedly, he lifted his hand again to assist Barbara to step down from the carriage, though he continued to speak to Catrine as he did so.

Barbara held gently to his fingers, afraid that he would detect the trembling of her hand. She felt the same magnetism as she had on the previous occasion and couldn't prevent a small gasp escaping her lips — which achieved the opposite of her desire. Lord Rockfort turned his attention to Barbara.

'Is anything amiss?' he asked, his tone concerned. He held on to the tips of her fingers and Barbara could feel herself blushing under his close scrutiny.

'No . . . No, m'lord. I am sorry. I . . . ' She cast around in her mind for a possible excuse for her involuntary reaction. 'I . . . er . . . thought I saw a rabbit running into the bushes over yonder.'

One eyebrow rose in mild amusement. 'A truly extraordinary occurrence,' he agreed. 'I trust the sight of a deer will not give you the vapours and send you screaming back to the carriage?'

Barbara blushed further in annoyance with herself at her ridiculous statement.

She was now standing beside him and tried to remove her hand but, for some unaccountable reason, Lord Rockfort refused to release her.

She glanced towards Philip and Catrine who were now many yards ahead of them. 'Should we not be following Mademoiselle Azaire and your cousin? This is my first outing as her chaperon and I would not like to fail in my duty towards her.'

Lord Rockfort followed her glance. 'You are quite right, Miss Chesney. I stand corrected and I apologise for keeping you from your duty.'

As he spoke, they both turned naturally in the direction of where Catrine and Philip were walking and Lord Rockfort at last released her hand. Barbara's heart was beating fast and for a few moments neither of them spoke. Barbara felt overwhelmed by his nearness to think of anything sensible to say and feared she would sound like a gauche schoolgirl if she attempted to speak.

She became aware that Lord Rockfort was regarding her quizzically and she forced herself to meet his gaze with an enquiring smile.

'Excuse me if I intrude into your private life, Miss Chesney, but tell me more about your parents. The name of Chesney is somewhat unusual . . . yet I have heard of it before.'

'Really? As far as I know, I have no family. My father was an only child.' She gave a small deprecating laugh as she added, 'And I don't think his family were of any consequence.'

Lord Rockfort looked at her coolly. 'And you think I would only be interested in people 'of consequence'?'

'Yes. That is, no.' Barbara felt confused. 'I don't really know. I just thought . . . ' She suddenly grinned impishly. 'I'm sorry! I'm making a fool of myself, aren't I? Have I offended you?'

'Not at all.' Lord Rockfort laughed agreeably. 'I am not offended. In fact, I find your natural way of speaking to be somewhat refreshing. Believe me, I am constantly besieged by a never-ending trial of position-seeking mammas and their simpering daughters who have nothing beyond their schoolroom talk to assail me with.'

Barbara was unsure whether to be pleased that he found her to be different or disconsolate that he obviously discounted her of being one who might lay claim to his heart.

'That's what comes of being regarded as a 'good catch'!' she laughed without thinking, instantly berating herself for her lack of delicacy.

Lord Rockfort laughed at her remark. 'An unenviable position for any man to be in,' he agreed. 'But I will make up my own mind . . . as you yourself have already done,' he reminded her. 'Tell me more about your father, Miss Chesney.'

This conversation was becoming too personal and she was sure that it was also quite irregular. Did he always catechise other people's household staff? Or was it because he intended to court Catrine and wished to vet her closest servant?

As she hesitated, she heard Catrine laugh at something Philip had said and was spared answering that or any further questions when Catrine suddenly stopped walking and came running lightly towards them.

'Lord Rockfort!'

She remembered her manners and dropped into a curtsey. 'Monsieur! Philip has just asked if I may attend the Assembly tomorrow evening.' Her face was alight with pleasure at the thought. 'Oh, please, monsieur le comte, do say I may!'

Barbara glanced at Lord Rockfort. There was a severity to his expression. Was he regretting letting his cousin spend so many moments alone with his intended conquest whilst he had been quizzing her?

Catrine's pleading expression was enough to melt the hardest of hearts and, as far as Catrine was concerned, Barbara knew Lord Rockfort's heart was ready to be melted.

'I will speak with Lady Birchley,' he promised. 'You will be carefully chaperoned and so I see no problems. But now, it is time to return to your carriage, Mademoiselle, or the London tongues will be wagging at the length of time I allow my young cousin to partake of your company.'

Was he curtailing his cousin's monopoly of Catrine? Barbara wondered. But his bland expression masked his inner thoughts.

Barbara expected Catrine to be disappointed at having her carriage ride cut short but she showed no sign of pique. 'We must spend the afternoon choosing what to wear, Barbara,' she gaily chattered as they were handed back into the carriage.

Philip took the reins again and, with his cousin there to curb his exuberant driving style, he directed the horses into a gentle turn before giving them rein along the return route.

Barbara was conscious of Lord Rockfort's presence as he rode alongside the carriage, conversing mainly in French with Catrine. It gave her time to sort out her own feelings and try to quell the fluttering in her heart that the lord caused.

Lord Rockfort escorted them as far as the tall wrought iron gates of Carlton House, where he gallantly lifted his hat in farewell before riding off to wherever his next business of the day required him to be.

Barbara was conscious of a fall in her spirit as he left

4

There was no holding Catrine back from beginning to plan what to wear for the ball, and the remainder of the day passed in a whirl of excitement as she scattered the contents of her wardrobe upon every available space.

Lady Birchley was to be the main chaperon but she allowed Barbara to accompany them. 'You will sit behind the chaperons with Annie, Barbara, but keep alert and watch how the chaperons conduct themselves and then you may be able to replace me at some future events. I have given Annie the task of selecting a suitable gown for you and she will help you with your hair.'

They rode in their own carriage, Lady Birchley considering it too public an event to allow Catrine to arrive escorted by a gentleman. Alfie was in high spirits. It was his first outing standing on the rear step and was swaggering about in his brand-new red and gold livery, though Will, the main coachman, was in charge.

The dances began and Catrine soon had her card filled up by eager young hopefuls. Lady Birchley made sure that conventions were adhered to and no-one was allowed more than two dances with her young charge. 'No, not even you, Philip,' Barbara overheard her say. 'Catherine must be launched upon the social scene with complete propriety.' She looked around the crowded ballroom through her lorgnette. 'Is your cousin, Lord Rockfort, here tonight, Philip? He had promised his support.'

'He will be here shortly, M'Lady. I believe he has some . . . er . . . business to attend to before he comes.' Philip seemed to give her a significant look, an expression that wasn't lost on the lady.

'Ah!' She nodded slowly. 'Of course! Say no more.'

The eventual sight of him approaching the group made Barbara's heart thump uncomfortably. He was dressed in dark red, with an elaborate band of gold embroidery around the front edges and cuffs of his coat. His satin breeches fitted tightly over his strongly-muscled thighs. She only realised that she was staring at him when his eyes met hers as he lifted his head and looked over the top of Catrine's head at her. She saw a slight frown pucker his eyebrows and he hesitated in drawing Catrine to her feet.

When the supper dance was announced, the ballroom began to empty, and Annie touched her arm. 'We can retire to a room at the rear for a few minutes whilst our mistresses are otherwise engaged.'

Because of the crush of ladies' maids, Barbara soon lost sight of Annie amidst the throng and after a refreshing drink of lemonade, unsure of how long she had been there, she hurried back towards where she supposed the ball-room to be. However, as she entered an ante-room by mistake, she saw Lord

Rockfort talking to a man dressed in black.

The difference in their apparel was matched by their difference in manner. The sombrely-dressed man was speaking sharply in words that Barbara couldn't understand, but she recognised the language as being French. Feeling a shiver of apprehension run through her, she drew back behind a pillar.

She saw Lord Rockfort flick nonchalantly at his sleeve, as though removing a speck of dust. 'La, Monsieur Lescarabé! You overestimate my ability to understand your language! I'm a mere beginner, I assure you.'

'Lesabre!' the man hissed. 'My name is Lesabre!'

'Ah, indeed!' Lord Rockfort held his lorgnette to his eyes, his expression disdainful. 'Speak plainly, sir, or I fear you speak in vain.'

'You surprise me, Lord Rockfort! I thought you to be an accomplished linguist!'

Lord Rockfort laughed in an affected manner, Barbara thought, her brow creasing in perplexity. What was he up to? And why was this unpleasant man speaking to him in such an abrupt vindictive manner?

Impulsively, deciding that a distraction was probably what Lord Rockfort needed, she stepped forward before she had time to think better of it and dropped into a low curtsey. 'Lord Rockfort! My mistress has been looking for you. She needs your immediate assistance, m'lord.'

Lord Rockfort looked startled for a moment but recovered admirably . . . well before his adversary. 'Then I had better seek her out. If you will excuse me, sir.' He made an elegant leg, flourishing his hand extravagantly as he bowed low, murmuring, 'Monsieur Lescarabé.'

The other man responded in a less flamboyant manner, his eyes cold and narrowed, diffusing pure malevolence. 'Lesabre!' he hissed once more.

Barbara shivered. She instinctively disliked him and was glad to turn her back on him, though she wasn't sure it was correct etiquette to do so. 'She is in an ante-room off the ballroom, m'lord,' she added helpfully, anxious now to be away from the man.

He gripped hold of her elbow and propelled her forward in the direction of the ballroom, from where the musical strains of 'Greensleeves' were drifting on the air.

'What the devil was all that about?' he hissed, as soon as they were out of earshot of the man. They were on the fringe of other revellers and Lord Rockfort slowed his pace, bowing to his right and left in brief acknowledgement of other greetings.

His grip on her elbow lessened but wasn't released. He hustled her into a deserted ante-room, closing the door behind them without releasing his hold.

'I take it that wasn't a genuine request for my presence,' he abruptly stated rather than asked.

Barbara was beginning to doubt the wisdom of her action. 'I didn't like the man,' she stated boldly. 'He was trying to trap you in some way.'

'And you think me incapable of taking care of myself?' he drawled carelessly, reverting to his earlier languid characterisation, his eyes narrowed slightly as he studied her face. 'A slip of a girl . . . ' He reached out and fingered the dark green satin of her puffed sleeves. ' 'My Lady Greensleeves' rescues me from . . . from what, precisely, were you rescuing me, I wonder?'

'I . . . ' She was suddenly uncertain. 'I don't know. I thought maybe he meant danger to my mistress.'

His eyes suddenly narrowed. 'Do you often eavesdrop on your betters? What game are you playing, I wonder?'

Barbara drew herself up tall. She raised her eyes and boldly met his stare. 'I was not eavesdropping! I was on my way back to Mademoiselle Azaire. And I was not the one playing games, m'lord,' she belatedly accused him, remembering his affected manner.

'Not playing games, eh?'

He suddenly reached out his hand and took hold of her chin. She was startled but was determined not to show it. She felt more indignant than afraid. He wouldn't treat Catrine like this, she'd wager!

'Unhand me, sir! You treat me discourteously!'

He laughed. 'Unhand you? Treat you discourteously? What words are those from a lady's maid?'

Barbara flinched at his tone, not realising that her uncertainty gave her face a vulnerable look.

Lord Rockfort caught his breath. This maid had already intrigued his mind and she suddenly looked very kissable. Before he knew what he was doing he had lowered his head and covered her moist pink lips with his own. Her initial start was predictable. He expected no less . . . but, as his kiss deepened, he was aware of a melting of her body as it moulded to his. A tiny moan from deep within her mouth fuelled his momentary lapse from gentlemanly behaviour and fanned it into a desire for more.

An unbidden joy coursed through him and caught him unawares. It was a sensation totally foreign to him. He was normally in full control of his desires and only dallied where reason led. But, now, he felt . . . protective . . .

However, Barbara's reaction to his kiss also rekindled his suspicion that she had been eavesdropping. Why was she here? Had she manoeuvred her way in Lady Birchley's household for some reason? Some reason that meant danger to Catrine? Yet, she had rescued him from Lesabre's poisonous clutch.

He was aware that he was functioning on two different levels — his head was reasoning . . . but his body was spiralling out of control. This had to stop before . . . before . . . before what? It was already too late!

He pushed her from him, holding her

at arm's length, his face inscrutable, revealing nothing of the turmoil within.

Barbara's senses were bewildered. Her body had surrendered in a way she had never imagined possible. She had felt totally at one with him . . . merged soul with soul, body with body. Yet, he, a gentleman, had treated her as a strumpet. How dare he? She had done nothing to deserve such treatment!

She again drew herself tall. 'As I said before . . . unhand me, sir!' she said coldly. 'I wish to return to my mistress.'

'What?' He seemed dazed. 'Yes, of course.' He released his hold of her. 'My apologies, Miss Chesney. I forgot myself. I am sorry.'

Never had Barbara seen him so discomposed . . . but she felt humiliated. She took two steps backwards, her fingers spread across her lips. Then, as her breath caught in her throat, she turned and hurried away.

Annie flung Barbara a dark look as she slipped into the seat beside her, suspiciously eyeing her flushed face. 'I hope you haven't been doing what it looks like you've been doing!' she hissed accusingly.

'I'm sorry!' Barbara whispered. 'I was delayed.' Had she been seen? 'Lord Rockfort had need of me . . . er . . . an errand . . . it was nothing!'

'Hmph! Lord Rockfort can run his own errands! You are Miss Catrine's maid, remember! Not his! Not yet, anyway.'

'What do you mean?'

'I shouldn't really say . . . but I overheard him speaking to Lady Birchley about becoming betrothed to Mademoiselle Azaire but my mistress said it was too soon . . . that she wants Mademoiselle Azaire to enjoy the London Season before she becomes betrothed.'

Barbara didn't know why it hurt so much to hear it. She had expected it, hadn't she? Though Barbara thought her also taken with Lord Rockfort's cousin, Philip. Still, she grimaced, when did personal preferences enter into it

67

with the highly born?

From Catrine's success tonight, there might be many such offers . . . but none would come much better than Lord Rockfort.

Barbara wondered how she would fare the next time Lord Rockfort came to call on her mistress — but she needn't have worried.

Whilst she was brushing out Catrine's hair the following day, fashioning it into Catrine's favoured ringlets, Catrine sighed dramatically. 'Hey-ho! We will not be seeing the handsome Lord Rockfort for a day or so, Barbara.'

'Oh?' Her heart began to thump alarmingly. 'Why is that?' she asked, as casually as she could.

'He is busy!' She met Barbara's eyes in the looking glass. 'He has gone . . . away.' In spite of her subdued tone, Catrine's eyes gleamed with suppressed excitement and Barbara suspected that she wanted to say more.

'Away where?' she obligingly asked.

Catrine turned around on her stool

to face her. 'He has gone to France!' she whispered dramatically, her fingers spread across her chest.

'Oh?'

'Oui,' he calls it his 'smuggling run'!'

Smuggling? Was that his game? Smuggling French brandy and other spirits into the country? She felt compelled to warn Catrine. 'You know that what he does is illegal?' she said quietly. 'And very dangerous!'

Catrine nodded soberly. 'I know! But we must not talk about it! Even speaking of it could lead him into danger! He is such a brave man!'

'Hmm! Brave and foolish!' Barbara snapped, her inner fear for his safety making her uncharacteristically abrupt. To hide her agitation she attacked Catrine's curls again with renewed vigour, her lips firmly pressed together to hide her own fear.

'Some might say foolish, Barbara . . . ' Catrine said quietly, ' . . . but I only see his danger.' She clasped her hands firmly across her chest again, this time in earnest. 'I will be heart-broken if anything should happen to him!'

Barbara was immediately contrite. 'Oh, I'm sorry, Catrine! I wasn't thinking straight. Of course you will. Forgive me for being so insensitive.' She stooped down and hugged Catrine's shoulders. 'The days will soon pass, I'm sure.'

'Yes! And, in the meantime, we must act as though nothing is wrong!' Catrine said bravely. 'I wonder if Philip will call today? He will help to distract us, won't he?'

'Of course, he will.' She wondered if Philip minded being a decoy for his cousin. He didn't seem to. She was sure he held a few romantic notions about Catrine, anyway. And it would serve Lord Rockfort right if Philip displaced Catrine's affections from Lord Rockfort to himself. Smuggling, indeed! The man had no need of the money! He was doing it simply for the excitement. And risking breaking Catrine's heart, in the bargain.

Her thoughts were later distracted from Catrine and Lord Rockfort when Lizzie, one of the kitchen maids, tentatively knocked on the door of the music room, where Catrine was playing beautifully on the piano. It was some hauntingly sad music that Barbara felt was releasing some of Catrine's pent-up anxiety over her beau.

Lizzie seemed confused and bobbed a curtsey to both girls.

'Yes, Lizzie?' Barbara asked. 'Have you a message for Mademoiselle Catrine?'

'No, Miss. It's for you! It's a young . . . woman . . . a girl, really. She's in the kitchen.'

'Didn't she give her name?' Who could it be? 'Is it all right if I go down to see who it is, Catrine?'

'But, of course, Barbara.'

Barbara hurried after the retreating figure of Lizzie down the staff stairs to the kitchen, her mind running ahead of herself.

None of her thoughts had come

anywhere near to the truth. To her utter amazement, it was Amaryllis who awaited her!

Barbara halted in amazement. 'Amaryllis! What are you doing here?' A sudden apprehension seized her. 'Oh, no! It's not my uncle or aunt, is it? Has something happened to one of them?'

'And what would you care if it had?' Amaryllis said coldly. 'You care little for either me or my family! No! I have come to demand that you return to us now that we are in residence here in London for the Season. We are finding it very difficult to manage . . . and it won't do!' Her voice had grown shrill.

Barbara felt embarrassed. She glanced apologetically to the kitchen staff, grimacing her lips slightly. 'Come and sit down, Amaryllis.' She indicated a chair by the kitchen table.

Amaryllis ignored the invitation. 'I have no time to sit, Barbara. Go and get your things . . . whatever you've got . . . and come with me at once. If you have to be a lady's maid, you might as well be mine! I cannot abide the one Mamma has engaged for me! She pulls my hair so and refuses to pick up my clothes!' She narrowed her eyes and lowered her voice. 'If you give me back my ruby ring, I will tell papa that I have found it in a drawer.'

Barbara drew in her breath. 'You wouldn't consider telling Uncle Walter that you actually gave me the ring?'

'Well, no. I mean, how could I? I have already told him you stole it. He would be angry with me if he knew I had given it to you. If you won't come, I shall tell everyone here that you are a thief!'

Barbara's face whitened. 'Amaryllis! You know I didn't steal your ring!'

'It's your choice, Barbara!' Her eyes remained fixed on Barbara's face, triumphant now. She paused, tapping her foot as she waited for Barbara's response.

Barbara drew in her breath sharply, her mind racing. What option had she? Her life would be in ruin, whichever she chose.

5

'May I ask what is happening here?' Lady Birchley's voice spoke quietly from the kitchen door. 'I have been ringing the bell for some minutes and I find you all here, listening to this scurrilous gossip!'

Everyone's attention swung from Amaryllis to the mistress of the house. Cook made a movement to speak, but Lady Birchley signalled her to remain silent.

Amaryllis coloured slightly but thrust her chin forward. 'I am Amaryllis Marchant and I have come to take my cousin home,' she said, her voice now a trifle defiant. 'She is needed there.'

'But is she welcome there?' Lady Birchley asked quietly. 'Here, she is both needed and welcome.'

Amaryllis tossed her head. 'You obviously don't know my cousin very well, Madam!' Her eyes narrowed. 'Do you know why she ran away from my father's loving care, distressing him greatly?'

'I know the two reasons your father gave, Miss Marchant, but I would wager you know differently!'

The emphasis on the word 'you' and the expression in her eyes momentarily wilted Amaryllis's bravado but she made recovery. 'A costly ruby ring went missing!' she insisted on adding, a thin smile tightening her lips. 'But we have generously decided to overlook the occurrence. As to the other matter, it is no longer an issue. Squire Bailey has withdrawn his offer.' She turned back to Barbara. 'So, you see, cousin, there is no barrier to your immediate return.'

Barbara paled at the insinuation of her implication in the ring's loss but she courageously stood firm. 'You know I did not take the ring, Amaryllis! Besides which, I choose to remain here where my service is valued. Give my regards to my aunt and uncle. I wish them well.'

Amaryllis looked furious. 'Don't think our offer will remain open for long. I shall insist my father takes the matter further. You'll be sorry you spurned our generosity!'

Barbara felt her knees weaken. Was Amaryllis threatening her with action from the authorities? She shot an anguished glance at Lady Birchley.

Lady Birchley smiled grimly. 'I think, Miss Marchant, you need to speak of this matter with your father. He obviously knows nothing of your intention to come here today. I marvel at the impropriety of your action. Now, I demand that you leave. My household has been disrupted enough for one day! Good day to you!'

Amaryllis's face reddened. After a momentary pause, she swung on her heels and stalked out of the kitchen, letting the outer door slam as she passed through it.

Barbara felt shaken.

Lady Birchley took command. 'Well, the show is over for today,' she said brightly. 'I wish you all to know that there is no foundation in any of Miss Marchant's remarks. She has been a spoiled child who is too used to having her own way . . . and beguiles her father too readily! Should the young lady return, Mrs Pawley, do not invite her inside. Come, Barbara. Mademoiselle Catrine is ready for you to dress her hair.'

Grateful for her intervention, Barbara followed her out of the kitchen and up the steps. 'Thank you for standing by me, Lady Birchley. I really didn't steal her ruby ring.'

Lady Birchley laid her hand on Barbara's arm. 'If I, for one moment, suspected that you had, I would not have taken you into my employment, Barbara. I pride myself on being a good judge of character. I wasn't going to tell you this but my confidence in you is such that, when I went to see your aunt and uncle last week, I recompensed them for the alleged loss . . . No, no! Say no more! I understand.' She frowned slightly. 'Your cousin is the product of too-indulgent parents. I didn't like the malevolence in her eyes. Take care, Barbara, in any dealings you may have with her. She bodes you no good.'

Barbara repeated little of the incident to Catrine as she dressed her hair, not wishing to upset her on her behalf. Catrine had already planned the rest of the day, having received a note from Philip that he intended to call that afternoon to escort her in a ride to Richmond Hill.

'I have sent word to Will that Alfie may accompany us,' she added. 'Philip has not got the livery boy today, as you call him. He fell off the carriage! Alfie will be very pleased, oui?'

'Yes!' laughed Barbara. 'Alfie will be pleased!'

He was! As proud as a peacock, he stood on the rear step of Philip's phaeton as they bowled along through the London streets.

Only one event marred the outing.

They were bowling along at a fair speed on their return journey when a larger carriage, a closed barouche, cut across their path at a deserted junction, almost causing a spill.

The two ladies screamed as the two vehicles all but touched. It was only Philip's driving skill that avoided what could have been a nasty accident.

Philip drew in the reins and leapt from his seat as soon as his horses were back under control and drawn to a halt. Alfie leapt down also and ran forward to hold on the horses' bridles, talking to the startled beasts in order to calm them.

The hired barouche, for that is what it was, hadn't halted. The much caped-and-collared driver, a tall-crowned beaver hat hiding most of his facial features, had urged his horses on as soon as the two vehicles had evaded collision.

Philip shook his fist at its retreating image. He turned to the ladies. 'My apologies, ladies!

'Non, non! You were formidable!' Catrine praised, mixing French words with English in her agitation. 'I am so proud of you!'

'Yes, well done, Mr Grafton,' Barbara added, feeling badly shaken.

Philip coloured modestly. 'It was nothing,' he demurred, beaming all the same. 'But it could have been a serious accident! No wonder the fellow didn't stop! I'd have called him out if I'd had the chance!'

Barbara paled, thankful that Catrine was unfamiliar with the phrase. 'Oh, no, Mr Grafton! No! Please! Not on our account. No, we are simply gratified that no harm was done, aren't we, Catrine?'

Catrine held out both of her hands towards Philip by way of giving thanks.

He seized hold of them and lowered his lips to brush them lightly. 'The honour is mine,' he assured her. 'Are you well enough to continue home, ladies?'

'We are fine, Mr Grafton,' Barbara

assured him, looking rather pointedly at his two hands that still enveloped Catrine's smaller ones.

He blushed and withdrew them, taking his seat once more. 'Let 'em go, Alfie!' he called.

Barbara's heart within was still beating fast and her mind disturbed. Though she wasn't sure enough to speak of it, she felt she had recognised the glimpse she had had of the face of the barouche's passenger. It was Monsieur Lesabre, the mean-faced man whom she had seen talking with Lord Rockfort at the ball, the man from whose presence she had felt obliged to rescue his lordship.

Had the incident been an unfortunate near accident? Or did it have more sinister tones? Barbara wasn't sure . . . but she couldn't help feeling perturbed by it.

None of them mentioned the incident to Lady Birchley on their return, though there had been no verbal agreement not to do so. Barbara didn't want to cause unnecessary worry on such slender suspicions and she suspected that Catrine and Philip did not wish to have Lady Birchley's sanction to their outings withdrawn. Catrine might well be unofficially betrothed to Lord Rockfort, but it was evident to her maid that she also enjoyed the court paid her by the younger of the two cousins.

Some cards had been left on a silver tray on the hall table whilst they were out. Catrine was highly delighted with them.

'It means I can receive them as visitors,' she explained to Barbara, who was, as yet, unfamiliar with the social etiquette involved in leaving cards. 'No-one can visit until their card has been received. Now, I can leave my card. Then my visitors can visit, but for no more than ten minutes . . . or maybe a little longer if no-one is there to see it!' She grinned impishly.

Lady Birchley gave permission for Catrine to leave cards the following afternoon. Will was their coachman and Alfie once more rode as livery boy. It was a pleasant afternoon's drive and all the cards had been received, much to Catrine's delight.

Heavy rain kept them indoors the next two days. Barbara was pleased to discover that Catrine enjoyed doing tapestry work and they decided to work on two identical covers for some cushions. They eagerly sorted out some coloured threads from Lady Birchley's well-stocked workbox, and agreed upon the pattern they were to copy. The inclement days thus passed swiftly and the following day, the day of the promised visit, some of the previous card-callers, dawned brightly.

The second footman bowed each visitor into the room, and Barbara was kept busy helping to assemble trays of tiny sandwiches and small cakes in the kitchen and carrying them upstairs as and when needed.

A number of young men made their call, all seemingly intent on catching the eye of the pretty young French girl.

Barbara wasn't sure when Lord Rockfort arrived. However, she saw a sudden look of delight lighten Catrine's face and she turned to see the cause of it. He was there!

Her own heart leapt with joy, so she knew exactly what Catrine was feeling. There was an unspoken message in exchange of glances. She felt a surge of jealousy, wishing it were herself who was on the receiving end of Lord Rockfort's special glance. He must love Catrine tremendously to send such a glance her way!

He was dressed in his riding clothes and made formal apology, excusing his attire on his late arrival from travel. 'I was anxious to remake your acquaintances this afternoon. My man was scolding me all the while!'

Barbara noticed he had had time to change into immaculate cream-coloured breeches and highly polished riding boots, none of which had seen recent travel to France.

The splendour of his form made her heart lurch with desire. Her breath caught in her throat as she drank in the sight. She was sure she hadn't made a sound . . . but his eyes caught hers as he straightened . . . and they locked together. It seemed an age before either looked away, though Barbara couldn't think of any reason for it to have been so.

Out of the corner of her eye, she could see him engage in conversation with a group near the temporarily abandoned tapestry frames of the previous two days. She heard Catrine exclaim something and glanced over to see her animatedly describing some of the finer points of the craft to the courtly crowd.

Lord Rockfort stood to one side, smiling faintly as he listened. The other young men were making open court, each, no doubt, assured that his was the one making most impact. Was he amused at the others' antics? Or did he feel a similar jealousy to that in her own heart?

A faint touch of warm breath against her neck startled her and alerted her to someone's presence close behind her. She knew who it was, of course! The prickles running along her spine gave her the answer. Even so, she couldn't restrain the slight gasp that escaped her lips as she turned round and found his face almost touching hers.

Lord Rockfort smiled in amusement, it seemed. He nodded towards the window. 'A very impressive view,' he drawled. 'I wondered what could be so engrossing that it kept you from acknowledging Mademoiselle Catrine's praise of your exquisite tapestry work.'

Was he sporting with her? His close presence unnerved her. She made the mistake of raising her eyes to rest on his mouth. He was smiling and she could see the tips of his gleaming white teeth. Her insides melted. An evocative fragrance emanated from him. She couldn't name it but she knew she would always associate it with this man.

'Catrine's praise of my work is appreciated, m'lord . . . as mine would be of hers . . . but you must allow me some modesty, m'lord, however false it may be!' she replied with spirit, making a mock curtsey.

He laughed. 'Well said, Miss Chesney. Your delightful mistress champions your case most strongly.' He turned to glance in Catrine's direction, smiling at her animate conversation. 'But I must urge you, Miss Chesney, to be extremely vigilant in watching over Mademoiselle Azaire. I do not want anything untoward to happen to her.'

He lifted a hand and for a heart-stopping moment she thought he was going to tease out a curl and let it twine around his finger . . . but he didn't. He swivelled on his heel and turned the gesture into a laconic wave of his hand. 'Ha! George Worralson, I declare you are following me around town this day! Are you also here to pay court to the lovely Mademoiselle Azaire? I wager you will have a fight on your hands. There are at least a dozen suitors with a prior claim to ours!'

They made a fine leg to each other, then crossed the room to join another group of visitors. Barbara watched them go, mulling over the words that he had spoken. He obviously loved Catrine very dearly.

The trees in the park were splendorous in their summer dress as Philip drove them along the narrow roadway.

Whenever they had such an outing, Lord Rockfort was sure to appear at some point or other. Barbara had learned to relax in his presence and felt free to speak to him without being addressed first, though this was a privilege she only availed herself of when no outsiders were present.

'Lord Rockfort!' she greeted him with on this fine day. 'I declare that you either spend all your days riding around the park . . . or you come by special arrangement when we are here!'

Lord Rockfort doffed his hat, maintaining perfect balance on his black stallion.

Catrine was seated beside her, whirling a pretty parasol over her shoulder. 'I think it is a special arrangement.' She smiled. 'We do seem to see quite a lot of you, my Lord Rockfort!'

'I like to keep an eye on my special ladies!' he gallantly replied, bowing gracefully. He smiled suddenly, exchanging a glance with Catrine before saying, 'I have hopes of being able to convey some good news to you, Miss Chesney, before many days are past.'

'Oh?' Barbara felt her cheeks redden as his glance swept between both her and Catrine. He must be hoping to announce his betrothal to Catrine! She must learn not to mind.

After he had ridden away, Catrine laughed doltishly. 'Barbara! Your red cheeks betray your thoughts! You are as enamoured by Lord Rockfort as the rest of my friends!'

Barbara managed to laugh lightly. 'And no wonder! He is very handsome! He is enough to turn anyone's heart!'

'And what about Philip? Is he also enough to 'turn your heart'?' she asked coyly, looking at Barbara from under her thick lashes.

Barbara laughed also. 'He is very dashing . . . and he certainly is one of your willing slaves, Catrine!' She paused, not wanting to spoil the friendship between the two of them. 'Don't break his heart, will you, Catrine!'

Catrine sobered instantly. She took hold of Barbara's hand and looked earnestly at her. 'I will never break his heart, Barbara! We know what we are doing!'

Two days later Barbara received a sealed note, delivered by hand.

Lady Birchley had decreed that this was to be a quiet day with no visitors, so Catrine and Barbara were stitching their tapestries, happily chattering away about their outings in the park and the various visitors who had called in recent days.

Catrine was teaching a few French phrases to Barbara, laughing in merriment when she mixed up bonjour with au revoir.

The footman bringing in the note on a silver tray interrupted their laughter. He bowed stiffly before Barbara.

She looked up in surprise. 'For me?'

The footman bowed again, lowering the tray so that she could read her name on the folded sheet.

'Thank you, Forbes.' She picked it up and shrugged apologetically to Catrine. 'Whom can it be from? I don't know anyone who would presume to send a note to me at the front door.'

Catrine grinned. 'Open it, Barbara, then we shall know!'

Barbara was already slitting the note open with the edge of her scissors. She quickly scanned the paper, her left hand rising to touch her cheek as she did so.

'Is it bad news, Barbara?'

'I'm not sure.' She read the note

again, a frown puckering her forehead. 'It's from Amaryllis. You know, my cousin. She says she has something important to tell me and asks if I will meet her in the park straight after lunch. She says not to tell Lady Birchley because she knows she will prevent me from seeing her. She suggests we arrange to ride in the carriage and meet her by that little spinney across from the bandstand.'

She lowered the note, grimacing ruefully. 'I'm not happy about it, Catrine. I don't like to deceive Lady Birchley. She has been so good to me.'

'But your cousin is right,' Catrine pointed out. 'Lady Birchley would not receive her again. Maybe she has something to say about the missing ring? Maybe she wishes to confess that she gave it to you?'

Barbara thoughtfully considered the point.

'What harm will it do, Barbara?' Catrine persisted. 'Maybe your aunt and uncle wish to see you again? You will never know, if you do not go.'

Barbara sighed. 'Perhaps you're right. I just hate being secretive!'

'Then I will make the arrangements! I will ask Lady Birchley if we may ride in the carriage this afternoon.' She beamed across at Barbara. 'If I am there also, Amaryllis will not be unkind to you.'

'As you say, what harm can there be?' Barbara replied.

Permission was granted and after a light lunch the two young ladies dressed for the ride in the park. It was a cool, cloudy day.

'We must wear our cloaks,' Barbara decided.

'We will not see the handsome Lord Rockfort today,' Catrine teased

'No . . . and I don't suppose Will will drive as recklessly as Philip!' Barbara grinned back.

Alfie was pleased to be having another outing. 'I'm getting a dab hand at this, Miss Barbara!' he boasted, waiting until the carriage set off before grabbing hold of the handle and leaping on to the back step.

It was a pleasant ride. Not many other vehicles were about, as it was unfashionably early and the park looked deserted.

'There she is! By those trees,' Catrine pointed out.

Alfie had already lowered the step and they stepped down to the ground. Amaryllis's cloaked figure was no longer in view as Barbara and Catrine strolled across the grass.

'I hope she's not playing silly games!' Barbara exclaimed in exasperation. 'We didn't come here to play hide and seek!'

However, it seemed that that was Amaryllis's intention. The two young ladies paraded round the spinney, peering into the thicket of bushes and trees.

'I'll go inside and look, shall I, Miss?' Alfie offered, ready to bound in amongst the bushes.

'No!' Barbara spoke sharply. 'If Amaryllis is hiding from us, that is her look-out. Let's return to the carriage, Catrine. I knew we shouldn't have come. She is so silly at times.' She suddenly felt ill at ease, though she wasn't totally sure why.

Will's hunched figure on the driving seat straightened as they approached the carriage.

'We are returning home, Will,' Catrine ordered as she climbed up the step.

Barbara climbed up after her. Before she had seated herself, the carriage jerked forward, flinging her backwards against the seat.

The carriage was picking up speed. The horses were galloping swiftly, encouraged onwards by the cracking whip.

Barbara looked over her shoulder to make sure Alfie was on board. He was . . . but he wasn't smiling. 'That cove who's driving us ain't Will, Miss Barbara!' he hissed.

'What d'you mean, it ain't . . . I mean, if it isn't Will, who is it, then?'

'I dunno, Miss Barbara . . . but I reckon we've been kidnapped!'

6

'Are you sure, Alfie?' Barbara was filled with alarm. If it wasn't Will who was on the carriage, who was it?

'I caught sight of his ugly mug as he got into t'carriage, Miss . . . and it ain't Will!'

Catrine's face had paled and fear shone in her eyes. 'I have been captured!' she said quietly. 'Lord Rockfort warned me to be careful. He knew they might try.' She clutched hold of Barbara's arm. 'I am afraid, Barbara! They will take me back to France and kill me, like they did my parents. They never give up!'

Barbara gasped in horror at the thought. 'Oh, Catrine! And I'm to blame! And . . . Amaryllis!' The thought struck her heart coldly.

She shook her head. Such questions could be asked later . . . if there was a 'later' for them. They were in serious trouble. 'We shouldn't have come out like this on our own! No-one knows where we are!'

'You must not blame yourself, Barbara!' Catrine implored her. 'It was I who insisted that we come! But, I am still afraid!'

Barbara's mind was whirling round. Where was Will? Had he been killed? Or was he merely wounded and out of action? She knew that he would have done everything he could to prevent this terrible deed, so either of the eventualities was likely.

So, what could they do? They must be heading for the coast. How far was it to Dover? She searched her memory. About seventy miles, she thought. The horses couldn't go that far, not at this speed. They would have to stop some-where. Change carriages and horses . . . or would they go to the river? Whichever, once they were removed from their carriage, it would be harder to get away. They had to act now.

She looked at the hunched figure of the coachman. His caped cloak was pulled high around his face, obviously to hide his identify from them. She thought swiftly. If she could change places with Catrine, he might let Catrine go. They would have no interest in a servant maid.

'Quick, Catrine! Slip off your cloak and put on mine! Do it now!' She unfastened hers and slipped it from around her shoulders, helping Catrine to do the same. 'Pull the hood up! There!'

'But . . . why have we done this?' Catrine asked in bewilderment.

'They will have no interest in me. I would be just another mouth to feed . . . another person to guard. Therefore, you must pretend to be me!'

Catrine's face froze as she took in what Barbara was saying. 'But what about you, Barbara? What will they do to you? And how will you convince them you are me? The moment you speak, they will know you are not French!'

'I know a few words. I will bluff them!'

'You will not know what they have said.'

'I will tell them that I refuse to speak to them! Now, tell me, what is the French for, 'I will say nothing'?'

'Je ne parlerai rien!'

'Je ne parlerai rien! Je ne parlerai rien!'

'That's good!' Catrine reluctantly clutched at the faint hope Barbara was offering to her. 'You will need other words. Au secours! Means, 'Help!' '

'Au secours!'

Catrine stared at her, weighing her words. 'But, Barbara, they are very wicked men. They might kill you!'

Barbara swallowed hard. She knew it was a possibility . . . but she had no alternative. Hadn't she promised Lord Rockfort that she would protect his bride?

She pulled up her own hood and twisted round to face Alfie on the back step. 'Alfie, the driver might not realise that you managed to get on board! You must get Catrine somewhere safe! She is the one they are after . . . not me!'

She waited until he nodded. 'Right!' she swallowed again, fearful of her own safety. 'Once you are sure that Catrine is safe, you may try to rescue me . . . but only if it involves no danger to yourself! Promise me that!'

Alfie reluctantly nodded. 'I'll do me best, Miss.'

'I know you will.' She smiled fondly at him.

Abruptly, the carriage swung into a merchant's yard and the sweating horses were reined in to a trembling standstill. She clutched hold of Catrine. 'Be brave, Catrine, and do as we planned! It's our only chance!'

At the sound of their arrival, three rough seamen rushed out of the ramshackle building. One ran in front of the horses, holding them steady as the driver leapt down from his seat and tossed him the reins. The other two leaped into the carriage. They towered above Barbara and Catrine.

Both ladies instinctively cringed away from them. The men were fearsome to look at . . . and their coarseness of speech and attire instilled them with dread.

'Which one?' one of the men roughly demanded of their driver.

They were English!

Barbara knew she had to act fast. She gathered her cloak about her and stood up, putting on an air of high society. Imitating Catrine's accent, she said boldly, ''Ow dare you? What do you want with my maid and I? Let us go, immediately!'

The men roughly grabbed hold of her. 'We only want you, Frenchie!'

The horses pranced skittishly, as if they sensed danger. The carriage lurched and Barbara lost her balance, falling forward against her captor. He laughed as he half-carried, half-dragged her out of the carriage.

Barbara instinctively struggled, even though she intended to be the one who was taken. She remembered to cry, 'Au secours! Au secours!' Her fear was genuine.

Barbara's captor was dragging her backwards over the cobbles. She lost her shoes but barely felt the roughness of the stones scraping her heels. She was very frightened. What would happen to her?

They were in a dim building, some sort of warehouse, when the one who had abducted them spoke. 'Bind and gag her!' he ordered curtly. 'We need to catch the tide.'

'We've to get her aboard the barge without delay! Drag that crate over 'ere!'

Barbara was unceremoniously lifted by two of the men and swung none too gently into a wooden crate. She felt rough sacking underneath her and some more was dropped on top of her, casting her into darkness. She felt faint and nauseous . . . and terrified out of her wits but she mustn't reveal who she was! She must give Catrine and Alfie time to get away! Oh, Maximilian! Did he realise what a price he had asked of her?

The crate was lifted and deposited on to some kind of cart, jolting every bone in her body as it travelled over the cobblestones.

Barbara slipped in and out of consciousness, dreaming vividly of crazy chases and grotesque faces leering at her. Her head ached. Every muscle of her body screamed in agony. Tears rolled down her cheeks into the sacking.

The pitch and roll of the ship penetrated her consciousness and her eyes flew open. She was still at sea. A shaft of light was streaming into the room through a small round aperture. She was on the floor lying on bare wooden boards in some sort of small room. Oh! Her head! Her body! Every muscle! She pushed herself up, leaning on one hand and realised that she was no longer bound nor gagged.

She staggered to her feet, trying to

keep balance . . . but she was flung to one side. As she slithered to the floor again, the door opened and a dark-clothed man stepped into the cabin.

'Au secours!' she begged through cracked lips. What had Catrine said was French for water? Ah, yes. 'L'eau, s'il vous plait!'

A rapid sentence was volleyed at her. He hadn't a clue what it meant.

'L'eau!' she begged again.

The man grunted assent and soon the metal rim of a tankard was held to her lips. She greedily supped at the liquid, nearly choking as it hit the back of her throat. It was cheap wine. She coughed and sputtered and sank back to the floor.

'Merci!' she whispered hoarsely, wondering how long she could get away with speaking her very limited French. Did they still think she was Catrine? She had better assume so.

Another sentence was shot at her. She lowered the tankard. What was that phrase? Ah! 'Je ne parlerai rien!' she whispered, aware that her cracked lips wouldn't function properly — but maybe that was to the good. It would help to disguise her far from perfect accent.

At her refusal to speak further, the man opened the door and shouted an order. Two sailors appeared and hustled her out of the room, gripping her arms tightly.

She was thrust into a small dark room and the door was slammed behind her. She stumbled and fell headlong, adding more bruises to her battered limbs. Despair washed over her and she began to sob uncontrollably.

Hours later, after a long, wearisome voyage, Barbara sensed their arrival in France by the steadier motion of the ship. She heard the key being turned in the lock and she pulled up the hood of her cloak.

Light streamed in. All Barbara could see was a dark silhouette of a man framed in the bright doorway. He spoke some unintelligible words and a tankard was given to her.

'Merci!' she whispered hoarsely. She gulped it gratefully, feeling the liquid course down her throat to her stomach, leaving a burning trail. As the fire of the wine rejuvenated her limbs, a woozy sensation flowed through her head and she felt the world floating away.

The next two days passed in a haze of discomfort, pain and unfocussed unreality. Barbara was vaguely aware of being hauled from a coach and propelled into an inn, where a serving girl helped her. Bowls of broth were held to her lips while she gulped and spluttered as the hot liquid was poured into her. There was no taste to it but she neither demurred nor complained.

It was the noise that awakened her. An incessant clamour of human voices in a foreign tongue. She raised a hand to her head. It throbbed with pain. There wasn't much light . . . but the weak rays hurt her eyes and she closed them again.

She forced her eyes open again and pushed herself upright. She was in a crowded, open-barred cell with other such cells on both sides of hers and opposite. The man and women beside her were mostly silent, though one or two shouted back to the motley rabble on the other side of the bars.

Grim-faced, grey-skinned, ill-clad people shuffled past, their faces distorted with hatred, spitting out their verbal abuse at the poor unfortunates behind the bars.

Barbara stared at the shuffling line of people in a mesmerised fascination. She felt detached from the scene. It was nothing to do with her. These people didn't hate her. She, like them, was a servant . . . not an 'aristo', the word that dripped from their sneering lips.

She didn't realise that she had risen to her feet — or that she had pushed her way forward until she stood by the cell bars. She held out her hands in plea. Catrine's voice seemed to speak through her. 'Au secours!' she begged.

The jeering face of an ageless hag

grinned toothlessly at her, mimicking her words. 'Au secours! Au secours! Ooh la-la!'

The grin on the lined and haggard face brought a surge of bile from Barbara's stomach. She stood immobile, uncomprehending, her eyes glazed.

She wasn't pretending. Her state of shock made the whole scene incomprehensible. She felt herself being dragged back towards the rear of the cell, away from the taunting faces. Her self-appointed protector hoped the shock would remain and be the natural anaesthetic to what might befall her.

A while later, a commotion outside the row of cells drew Barbara's attention. It seemed to be an elderly woman, wheeling along an old truck rather like a box on wheels. An assortment of brushes and buckets dangled from hooks on its side.

The stooped figure stood by the opposite cell door, waiting whilst one of the guards took a bunch of keys from his belt. He shouted some words and the prisoners cowered to the rear of the cell. One was bidden to pick up the latrine bucket and carry it to the doorway, where the old woman took it from him, tipped it into her evil-smelling box and then handed it back.

She pointed her finger at the watching prisoners, cackling and chortling at them. Her gaze lingered momentarily on Barbara's shocked face.

As their eyes met, Barbara felt repulsed by her hideous appearance. One eye was pulled down and a vivid scar slashed across her cheek. Did nothing of beauty remain in this world-gone-mad? Did hatred turn everything ugly? With a sense of shock, Barbara felt that the old woman's eyes seemed to pierce into her soul. She stepped backwards, her hand to her mouth.

The old woman pointed straight at her, saying something that amused the guards. She turned away and picked up the handles of her truck, starting to wheel it over. The next moment the cart had overturned and the old woman lay beneath it amidst its foul contents. The guards jeered and cursed, finding it both amusing and disgusting.

'Oi! Levez-vous! Get up!' a guard shouted to the woman.

She struggled to her feet once more and tried to pick up the cart, hobbling about with a pronounced limp. A second guard kicked her rear, sending her sprawling again.

Barbara cried out in distress, the woman's plight over-riding her earlier revulsion. She crossed the cell and shouted, 'Aidez la femme!' It was all she could think of.

The guard leered at her, reaching through the bars to stroke her face, drawing an appreciative laugh from the other guards. The old woman joined in, pointing to Barbara. 'Vous! . . . ' followed by a rapid volley of French. Her meaning was made clear by her actions. She wanted Barbara to carry out the latrine bucket and help her pick up the brushes and swill out the floor.

Barbara stepped back in horror. She couldn't do it!

The grinning guards thought otherwise. One unlocked the gate, another stepped in and dragged her forward while another pointed a pistol at the other inmates.

The guards jeered.

Barbara proudly tossed back her head. Right! She'd show them!

She seized the brush and began to sweep the muck towards the old woman, who cackled in delight, imitating her actions in an exaggerated manner. When the task was completed, the old woman made a mock curtsey, encouraging, by gesture, the guards to do likewise, paying mock homage to their prisoner.

Barbara straightened her body and held her head high. Their mockery hurt but she wasn't going to let it show. A certain handsome face swam before her eyes, making them moisten with unbidden tears. Had Lord Rockfort been reunited with Catrine? Were they concerned for her? She had no hope of rescue . . . not from this horrendous place! Events had gone too far, too soon. There had been no official charge; no identification; no opportunity to declare herself English. She was anonymously thrown in with the herd to rot or perish, she knew not which.

The sound of whistling drifted through the cell-block.

Barbara listened, her eyes widening in amazement. The tune was 'Greensleeves'.

She frowned. It had been played at the Assembly Rooms. Had her thoughts of Lord Rockfort conjured the tune in her mind?

The sound had gone . . . but not the memory. She wasn't very brave and the thought of never seeing England again made her tears flow again.

She was still wearing Catrine's cloak, though it was now torn and spoiled. She slipped her hand into a pocket in the hope of finding a handkerchief to wipe her eyes. Instead, her fingers encountered a folded slip of paper. She pulled it out and opened its folds. It was difficult to read it in the poor light but she could just make out the words, *Be ready tomorrow*, written in a bold hand.

She stared at it. Had it been in the pocket all along? Was it a message from the lovelorn Philip, hoping to make an assignation with Catrine.

The thought of Catrine brought a leap of hope into her heart. Catrine had been rescued from this prison, or one very like it. How had it been done? She looked up past the listless prisoners resigned to their fate; past the prison cell bars to the opposite row of cells. There were only two tiny windows in the whole place and they were high and barred. There was a stout door at both ends of the centre aisle, with an armed guard at each door and two armed guards slowly walking up and down the aisle.

No-one could have put the note into

her pocket . . . unless it were one of the other prisoners. There were only six others in the cell now, five women and a sickly young man of about her own age. She had had no physical contact with them . . . and if it were one of them, why hadn't they just whispered the words?

Hope had stirred within her but it melted away. She was not of noble birth. Who would risk losing their life to save hers? And even if there were such a brave person, no-one knew she was here. Her fingers crumpled the note and she pushed it back into her pocket with a deep sigh.

Day drifted into night. Barbara's body ached. She spent the night dozing fitfully, listening to the moans of the sick boy. He was quiet now. The others were asleep. Barbara struggled to her feet and limped over to him. Even in the dim light from the burning torches high on the wall above the barred doors she could see he was dead.

A guard who was leaning against the

wall stirred himself. He yawned, rubbing his eyes as he came over to investigate. Barbara stood up, letting the guard see the dead boy. She spread out her hands and shrugged, the only way she had of communicating.

A babble of noise from the locked door to the left heralded the latrine woman's entrance. The guard shouted to her, beckoning her over as he searched for the correct key at his waist.

The woman trundled her loathsome cargo along the aisle and some verbal bargaining went on between the woman and the guard. Barbara couldn't help having some admiration for the woman. Her job might well be the lowest of the low but she didn't cringe before the guard.

As the guard opened the gate, the hideous woman gestured to Barbara to lift out the bucket. The other guards had approached, curious about the cause of the minor disturbance. They stood aside to let Barbara pass by with the bucket.

Two of the guards stepped inside the cell and picked up the body by its arms and legs. The prisoners were stirring, wondering what was happening. By the time they had opened their eyes properly, the gate was locked again, with Barbara in the aisle.

The whistling of the opening bars of 'Greensleeves' sounded again, just as one of the flaming torches suddenly went out, plunging the whole area into near darkness. Immediately, all the prisoners started to bang, stamp and shout, creating instant mayhem.

Barbara heard a voice in her ear. 'Tomorrow is here! Duck down and crawl into the side of the truck!'

7

'W . . . what?' Barbara was still holding the bucket . . . but it fell from her hands with a clatter. A hand on her head and another in her back pushed her down and forward. Barbara could feel the edges of the latrine truck with her hands but wasn't given time to think about it. She scrabbled forward on her knees, finding herself in a small, cramped space.

What was happening? That had been an English voice . . . and . . . surely her ears were playing tricks on her! Or was she going completely mad? It couldn't be! Lord Rockfort, couldn't be here! . . . Could he?

At once the truck began to move, bumping and banging over the uneven floor. Every time it stopped, Barbara held her breath. Was she discovered? She didn't know where she was going but it could only be better than this place!

The trundling ceased. Again, Barbara held her breath. Where was she? She had put her trust in a whispered voice. Was it an elaborate hoax to make sport of her? She could hear voices ... French voices.

More trundling. The pattern was repeated several times. Each time Barbara expected discovery ... but each time they trundled on.

At last, in a place of silence, the side of the truck was drawn back. Hands reached towards her. 'Come quickly, Barbara! There is no time to lose!'

It was Lord Rockfort's voice!

She crawled out painfully, her mind whirling. How . . . ? Hands steadied her and she gazed in shock at the hideous figure of the woman who emptied the latrine buckets. 'But . . . where is he? Where's Lord Rockfort? I heard his voice!'

'At your service, Miss Chesney!' said the harridan, speaking with the voice of

Lord Rockfort as the figure performed a courtly flourish. 'But, enough! Quick! Out of those clothes and get these on. There's no time to be modest.'

Barbara stared in uncomprehending shock. Her brain couldn't make sense of what she was seeing and hearing.

The voice was his. The knowledge of that broke into her state of paralysed fear and allowed her body to move. She ripped apart the buttons down the bodice of her gown, his hand steadying her as she stepped out of it. He pulled the shirt over her head and she struggled in to the trousers. They were slightly tight but the shirt covered the unfastened waistband.

The grotesque figure scooped up her discarded clothing and stuffed it into the latrine bucket in the truck, pushing it down with one of the brushes.

Barbara realised that her companion was holding a small pair of scissors in his hand. 'I hate to do this, Barbara . . . but I take no chances on these occasions. Your hair,' he added.

'Beautiful though it normally is, it has to go! Stand still.'

He swiftly hacked at her matted curls, dropping them to the floor, where they lay in a heap around her bare feet. He handed her a soiled red cap. 'Put that on. It's the latest fashion. Every good revolutionist wears one!' He scooped up the locks of hair and pushed them into the bucket with her gown.

His demeanour changed. 'You must not speak to anyone at all, Barbara. You are my mute nephew. I will try not to lean too heavily. And, remember . . . say nothing!'

Barbara nervously stepped with him out of the small storeroom into a dim passageway. Her bare feet were raw and bleeding and covered in unmentionable filth. She wanted to ask about Catrine and Alfie, but didn't dare. That would have to wait, as would a host of other questions that she wanted to fire at him.

She felt weak but steeled herself to

stagger along, taking strength and courage from the hunched figure she was supposedly helping along. How had he made himself so realistically ugly?

The sound of hooves and the heavy rumbling of cartwheels over the cobbles grew louder behind them. She glanced fearfully over her shoulder. Were they being chased already?

She could see a heavy horse-drawn cart approaching, led by two soldiers on horseback who were forcing the milling crowds out of the way, lashing out with their whips, clearing a passage for the vehicle.

'Over here!' Lord Rockfort hissed in her ear, pushing her towards the buildings that loomed up beside them. 'Keep your head down!'

Barbara was terrified. To have escaped but now to be captured was too much to bear. She didn't think she could cope with being taken back into the prison. With rising hysteria, she prepared to fling herself under the wheels of the cart. Lord Rockfort's heavy weight leaning on her shoulder prevented her from doing so.

She realised her whole body was shaking. He gripped her shoulder. 'Don't be afraid. They aren't after us! They have their captives.'

Barbara risked lifting her head as the vehicle passed within feet of them. It was a rough wooden, uncovered wagon. About a dozen men and women were standing in it, clinging to the sides as their bodies swayed with the uneven movement of the wagon. Their faces were grey — with both dirt and fear. Barbara didn't recognise any of them, though they might well have shared her prison cell.

Her trembling became uncontrollable as she realised that she might have been amongst them but for the brave man at her side. She raised her agonised face, not seeing the hideous mask, seeing only his eyes. They were soft with understanding.

She was relieved when they slipped down a side street, away from the place where the inhuman noise was seated. Only a few stragglers hurried in the direction from which they had turned, intent on watching the grisly spectacle in the Square.

It must have taken them half-an-hour to pass through the back streets of Paris. Time and again, Barbara marvelled at Lord Rockfort's boldness, his ready wit, his confident side-chat to people who passed any comment.

At last they turned into a narrow back entry and in through the back door of a building . . . a hovel of a place. Lord Rockfort unlocked a door and hustled her into a sparsely-furnished room. There was a small table, a cupboard, two rickety chairs and a palliasse.

'Welcome to my 'town house'!' he said quietly, a mirthless smile on his lips.

He assisted her to a chair and helped her be seated. 'We cannot stay here long. There may be a hue and cry for you. We must get out of the city before they close the barriers.'

He dropped down before her and gently lifted up her feet. 'You poor girl! You have suffered much in the past few days.'

Barbara felt tears brimming in her eyes. 'Is Catrine safe? And Alfie? Did they get back home?'

Lord Rockfort rose to his feet. 'Yes, praise God! Catrine is safe . . . thanks to you and Alfie. You two brave souls have my eternal gratitude!'

'Yet you still came for me?' Barbara marvelled.

'What else was I to do?' he asked lightly. He had turned away and began to peel off the rubber mask that covered his face. 'Damned glad to be rid of that!' he quipped.

It was pure joy for Barbara to see his real features once more. As she watched the transformation taking place in front of her, the realisation came to her that it was Lord Rockfort who had rescued Catrine . . . and countless others . . . from the revolutionists. He wasn't a smuggler of brandy and other contraband! How could she have thought so?

'You are very brave,' she said quietly, overcome by her sudden knowledge.

He bowed his head slightly, his eyes warm. 'Thank you . . . but I don't do it on my own. I have some excellent men helping me. All are very brave! Many of them live here. They risk more than I. They are in constant danger.'

'Why do they do it?'

'They love their country . . . and they know that this terrible bloodshed achieves nothing! They work . . . and risk their lives . . . for a better future. However, enough of this chit-chat. We must get on.'

He undid the door of a cupboard and took out a box. 'Here, I regain my real self,' he said lightly, dragging some clothes out of the box, 'but you, my love, must stay as you are. A ragged urchin lad is less conspicuous . . . and less likely to attract unwanted attention than the attractive woman I know you to be!'

Barbara heard the endearment he had used. It warmed her heart, though she knew, of course, that he was still thinking of Catrine.

He opened a drawer in the cupboard and took out a box of face paints and powders. Barbara watched, fascinated, as he altered his eyebrows and hair colour and added a scar that ran from eye to neck. He met her eyes in the cracked mirror. 'People remember the scar . . . but not the face,' he explained.

'How did you find me?' Barbara asked, suddenly anxious to know how he had achieved the impossible.

'I knew this would be where your captors were bringing you. I followed on the next tide and met my contacts. They knew of your arrival and had followed you to Paris . . . except it was thought that you were French . . . that you were Mademoiselle Azaire. How on earth did you manage to keep up the pretence?'

Barbara laughed, the first time in days. 'By keeping my hair hidden and remembering a few words Catrine has taught me. How did you know which prison block, which cell?'

'I renewed my part-time work as 'latrine woman', searching every cell until I found you. We had already learned that there was to be no trial. Sentence had been passed eighteen months ago. But, enough of that for now! We are not yet safe. We have to get out of Paris before nightfall!'

Barbara swallowed and nodded. She had begun to relax and wasn't sure she could bear to face more danger. Lord Rockfort noticed the slight tremor. 'Don't be afraid, Barbara. They can smell fear. They know it so well in themselves.' His eyes looked both dark and warm at the same time. He lowered his head and, for a moment, Barbara felt he was going to kiss her lips.

Her own lips parted, letting out a slight gasp . . . but he didn't kiss her. She could feel his warm breath on her lips but he didn't make contact. She felt him relax.

As he turned back to his make-up job he said lightly. 'Do you think you could call me my given name of Maximilian, Barbara? My title could land me in trouble.' He gave a short laugh. 'My name is very patriotic. I share it with one of the bloodthirsty revolutionists, Maximilian Robespierre. You may call me Maximilian or Max — but not Maxie, as my cousin, Philip, is wont to do.' He raised a quizzical eyebrow, as he dabbed some grey powder in his hair.

'I'll try.'

'Good! Now, on this next stage of our escape, I have hidden a small wagon.'

The streets were less crowded now. It must have been getting on towards noon, Barbara guessed, still hardly able to believe the day's events so far. 'Are we safe, now?' she asked hopefully. They were out of Paris and heading for the coast.

'Not quite. Just one more stop . . . then you can rest, my dear one.'

They travelled west for some miles. Maximilian was hoping to lure the chase toward Caen or Le Havre. Then he swung north, crossing the River Seine at Limay, before heading north again towards Gournay-en-Bray.

It was mid-afternoon when the wagon rattled into the rear courtyard of an auberge in Martagny, a small village south of Gournay-en-Bray.

He had been to the inn before . . . many times. An ostler led away the tired horse for a brush-down and some oats. The wagon was stored in a dilapidated barn and an enclosed carriage brought out to the courtyard in readiness for their departure.

Barbara was barely conscious. She felt hot and cold in turn. Burning with fever one moment; shivering with cold the next. Her head swam in continual motion as she tried to struggle to her feet.

Maximilian swooped her into his arms and carried her inside the inn to a good-sized upstairs room at the front of the inn. The innkeeper's wife soon had a fire roaring in the grate and brought up basins of hot water to bathe the young English lady's bruised and filthy body. She was astounded when Maximilian, now bathed and shaved, insisted on being the one to wash the lady's bleeding feet, but he did it so tenderly, gently stroking oil on them to soothe the sores, that there were tears in her eyes as she watched.

Barbara lay on the soft sheets almost unaware . . . except that it felt so lovely to be clean again. The spiky remains of her hair, doing their utmost to twist into tight curls, gleaming against the pillow, her feverish face burning hot.

Maximilian looked at her regretfully. 'I know you need to rest my love, but I daren't stay so near to Paris. We must press on.'

8

It took no more than fifteen minutes from their arrival, to when Maximilian flicked the reins over the pair of greys and turned the carriage out of the yard, leaving the innkeeper's wife to do all that was necessary to erase any evidence of their recent visit and departure.

Barbara was now clothed in a soft carriage gown of darkest blue, wearing a wig of brown ringlets upon her head. Maximilian, dressed in light beige breeches, silk shirt and cravat, dark green coat and many-caped cloak cut a dashing figure.

A couple of travelling boxes containing items of clothing suitable for an English Lord and his Lady were fastened to the back of the carriage.

Barbara was barely conscious, her mind and body taking refuge in delirium induced by her few days of deprivation.

Maximilian turned left and headed northeast to Songeons and Grandvilliers and then northwards towards the valley of the River Somme, pushing on, knowing that he needed to put some distance between them and the government agent he knew was hot on their trail . . . Vincent Lesabre.

He knew this area well. He had spent his childhood and youth here amongst his French mother's family, until the untimely death of his late father's unmarried elder brother had dropped an English title into his lap. He had crossed the channel to take up his title . . . to find himself totally unsuited to what he saw as a flippant, pleasure-seeking way of life among the upper echelons of society.

When the news of the arrest and imprisonment of his mother and two sisters had reached him, he had returned to France without delay . . . only to find he was too late. They had suffered the indignity and terror of a mock trial, during which no witnesses had been allowed to speak for them — only bribed perjurers to accuse them of fabricated misdeeds. They had been executed the same day.

The full horror had hit him hard. He recalled the day he had returned to his childhood home, distraught and inconsolable. The only person to greet him was Gerard, his childhood friend, who had also been absent on the dreadful day when his family was taken. Gerard's father had been killed in the affray. The rest of their household had been driven away and forbidden to return.

He and Gerard, fired by the tales of others such as themselves who had daringly rescued some of the despised aristocracy, covenanted to thwart 'Madame Guillotine's' thirst for French aristocratic blood. What those unnamed heroes had done, so would they!

In the course of their campaign, he had met bravery in many disguises, but the young woman, who was at this moment in his carriage, was the first he had known who had willingly taken the place of another — and he was determined to return her to her native land . . . and then . . .

He left his thoughts trailing in the air as he spurred on his horses, stopping only to rest and water them and give sips of water to Barbara. She was still feverish.

In the meantime, however, he had to get them both to safety before any pursuit caught up with them. He knew his enemy well. Their paths had crossed often during the past two years . . . too often for it to be believed to be by chance. Lesabre would have no definite proof of Barbara's masquerade as her mistress, nor of his involvement in her rescue . . . but since when did the revolutionists require proof?

The fields around him lay fallow. The neglect saddened him. This was rich farmland where crops had grown almost without the help of mankind:

the land that was rightfully his! He had often laboured alongside his tenant farmers at harvest time, a man in a line of men swinging their scythes in an age-old rhythm as they worked their way across the fields.

His nostrils flared. He could almost catch the scent of the newly cut grass or corn ... though none had been harvested here in the past two years. What a waste!

He knew just where to cross the River Somme, a few miles east of Abbeville: he knew every bridge and ford for miles along this stretch of the river. A mounting excitement arose in his breast, followed by a surge of joy as the once-proud gateway came into sight. He was home!

He expertly swung the carriage between what was left of the stone pillars. He had been here on numerous occasions recently and, with the help of Gerard's skill in carpentry, had put into place many imaginative 'repairs' to the desecrated and neglected building. He guided the horses on to the curved drive to the rear courtyard, where he leapt down from his seat and opened the double doors to what appeared to be a derelict stable.

A low whistle commanded the horses to walk forward into the stable and Maximilian closed the doors behind the carriage. He then ran to the far end of the stable and reached down behind an untidy pile of bales of straw. As he pulled a lever, the end wall of the stable split into two, both portions swinging back, straw and all, to reveal an inner sanctum.

A young man strode from an open doorway. 'Maximilian! Bienvenue!' he held wide his arms to welcome his friend.

'Gerard! Ça va? How are you, my friend?'

They clasped each other's shoulders.

'Ça va. I was getting worried about you!'

'Good fortune rode with us, Gerard. I will tell you about it all later.'

They unhitched the horses as they spoke. Gerard began to lead the horses into yet another inner stable, whilst Maximilian stepped towards the carriage door.

'Tell Pierre to remove any evidence of our arrival, Gerard. I must see to Mademoiselle Chesney. She is not well and needs a good night's sleep.'

'The rooms are prepared, Max. Give me half an hour and I will have some food ready for you.' Gerard hurried away, calling for his young son, Pierre.

Barbara stirred as Max laid her on a simple truckle bed in one of the small rooms that Gerard had prepared for them. Her eyes flickered open, blind terror reflected there. 'Where are we? What's happened?'

Maximilian wiped her forehead with a cloth dipped in cool water. 'You are safe, Barbara. We are in my former home. We will rest here for a few days, until you are fit to travel further.' He smiled tenderly at her. 'Do not worry any more.'

In the absence of any servants, Maximilian cared for Barbara better than any hired woman might have done, sponging her feverish head to reduce her temperature and holding a cup of clear soup to her lips, coaxing her to drink a small amount of nourishing liquid. He slept by her side for two nights, attending to her needs, confident that she would remember little of the details, even though she often murmured his name.

'You must call me Max,' he reminded her, gently cooling her cheeks. 'The revolutionists have no respect for any title, French or English!'

'Max?' She opened her eyes and smiled.

His heart flipped. She looked so young and trusting, her features gamine with her urchin haircut. He lowered his head and gently brushed his lips against hers, even though he had promised himself he wouldn't

Her lips moved responsively, a low moan sounded in her throat.

When he lifted his head, he knew she was fast asleep . . . though her lips were curved into a soft smile.

On the third morning, Barbara opened her eyes. She was in a darkened room with faint rays of light shafting into the room from a small, high window.

She raised herself on to her elbows and looked over the edge of the bed. She could see the form of a masculine body, wrapped in blankets lying on the floor at the side of her bed. His face was turned towards her.

'Max?'

Her voice was low, but he heard it and opened his eyes.

'Yes?'

He was instantly alert and pushed back the blankets as he raised himself.

'What are you doing there?' Her voice was puzzled.

He smiled. 'Sleeping.'

'But, why there? Isn't there a bed for you?'

He ignored the question, realising

139

what her questions revealed. 'You're better!'

She considered his words. 'Have I been ill?'

'A little . . . and very tired. Sip this water and I will bring you something to eat.' He handed her a cup, sitting on the edge of her bed, watching as she drank the cool liquid.

'Where are we?'

'In my home.'

An incredible joy filled her. 'In London?'

She knew at once, by the expression on Maximilian's face that her joy was premature.

'No.' His voice was gentle as he corrected her assumption. 'We are about fifteen miles from the coast of France.'

She silently took in the information, trying hard to look on the bright side of events. 'You got me out of that terrible prison, didn't you?' Her voice portrayed her wonder. She met his eyes frankly. 'I was so frightened.'

'You were very brave.'

She didn't deny it. It would have been churlish. 'What else could I have done? Catrine has become my friend. She is very precious to me and I love her.'

He smiled, his eyes also full of love. 'Yes, she is precious,' he agreed.

Barbara felt an overwhelming sadness. She had awakened feeling loved. She had heard words of love . . . but they were all in her dreams, the only place she would hear them.

She bravely kept the smile on her lips. It didn't matter. Once they were back in England, she would be with the two people whom she loved.

Once they had breakfasted, Maximilian shared his plan with Barbara. 'My success in rescuing my compatriots lies in the fact that I constantly change my appearance . . . and that of my companions.' He smiled. 'In what guise do you think we should now present ourselves?'

They were seated at opposite sides of the small wooden table where they had eaten. Barbara looked up to meet his eyes. They were dancing with merriment.

A thrill of desire ran through her but she sought to quell it. 'Father and daughter, do you think?' she suggested impishly.

Max pulled a wry face. 'I am not that elderly,' he protested lightly.

'But you are the master of disguises! I have already been your nephew.'

Max spread out his hands in a regretful gesture. 'Your days of impersonating a youth are over! Your voice is too sweet and, in the eyes of any man, you are a beautiful young woman!'

Barbara's heart performed a double somersault. 'Then I shall be your servant?' she hastily queried. 'I can be very demure.' She cast down her eyes ... but ruined the modest effect by glancing up through her lashes again, amazed at her own boldness. She felt she had known him forever.

Max appeared to be equally relaxed with her. He was grinning widely. 'I think not! No respectable man of my class would travel with a female servant, demure or otherwise! My name . . . and yours . . . would be forever ruined! And I do not wish that to happen!'

No, of course not. He was to marry Catrine as soon as Lady Birchley deemed the time suitable.

He reached across the table and took hold of her hands. His eyes searched her face as he considered his next words.

Barbara felt a tremor pass through her. His weathered hands dwarfed her pale-skinned ones. He gently rubbed his thumbs along the edges of her hands between her thumbs and her wrists, sending a fiery dart spiralling along her arms. Her lips parted as she gasped slightly, her cheeks blushing. Guiltily, she raised her eyes to meet his, not sure what she expected to see.

His eyes were as dark as the midnight sky, penetrating in their depths. All humour had fled. 'I am sorry! I have been teasing you, Barbara. The problem, however, is real. Whilst on a rescue mission, I always aim to present circumstances that are feasible.' He glanced down, as if watching the action of his thumb upon her . . . yet she knew he wasn't. He was gathering the words to tell her what his plan entailed . . . and, somehow, she knew what it was.

'We cannot hide ourselves for the next stage of our journey. At some point, we must re-emerge amongst other travellers . . . and the only acceptable state we can adopt is that of a married couple!' His eyes twinkled again. 'Can you bear to think of me as your husband, do you think?'

9

Barbara's heart somersaulted. 'My husband!' she echoed, shock registering on her face, even though she had known what he was going to say. It was her heart's desire!

Max pressed his thumb into her hands. 'Not for real,' he hastened to assure her. 'When there is any likelihood of anyone seeing us, we must act naturally together. Can you do that, do you think?'

Barbara didn't want to blush. It seemed so juvenile. But her inner thoughts of how delightful the pretence would be brought a rosy hue to her cheeks. 'I will try,' she promised faintly.

'Good! To avoid any discrepancies about our intimate knowledge of each other's taste and so on, I think we need to portray ourselves as recently married. What do you say?'

Barbara swallowed hard as she nodded. 'Yes,' she agreed quietly.

'There is one small detail.'

He undid the tiny ribbon at the top of the pouch and tipped the contents of the pouch into his hand. Two rings lay on his open palm. 'They were my mother's,' he said simply. 'She had time to hide most of her jewellery and we had faithful servants who retrieved it for me. Allow me.'

He reached for her left hand and held it gently in his, selecting her third finger and carefully sliding on the plain gold band. He then picked up the other ring. 'My mother always liked sapphires and this was her favourite ring. I will be honoured if you will accept it as a gift.'

Barbara gasped in genuine shock. 'I can't do that!'

'Why not?'

'Because . . . we are only pretending! I cannot! It wouldn't be right! Besides, what would Catrine think? Maybe she would prefer it if you gave your mother's ring to her?' All she was aware of was that he was still holding her hand, gently caressing the finger he was about to slip this second ring on to.

'My dear girl! If I choose to give a ring to Catrine, I will decide which one to give her . . . but it won't be this one! This one would be totally unsuitable!'

Barbara sighed inwardly. He would probably want to give Catrine a ring sparkling with diamonds, she supposed. Although this one was beautiful, maybe it wasn't as valuable as it seemed?

'Do you like the ring?'

Max's tone was sharp, edged with exasperation. He held the ring towards her, showing its beautiful setting of dark blue sapphires.

Barbara made herself look at it and then lifted her eyes to meet his. 'It's lovely,' she said quietly. 'It's quite the most beautiful ring I have ever seen.'

His expression softened. 'Then will you do me the honour of wearing it?' Max gently held her hand as he slid the ring on the same finger as the wedding ring. Her heart beat fast. She looked at him curiously. His eyes seemed deep blue this morning. Was the colour reflected from the sapphires on her finger?

She realised Max was still holding her hand across the table. As she watched, he lifted her hand to his lips and lightly kissed her fingers. His lips felt warm and as soft as velvet. She knew it was part of their pretence . . . but surely it didn't matter if she actually enjoyed it? People would expect to see some exchanges of love between them and it would do no good to their charade if she almost swooned every time he touched her!

Gerard's entrance into the room brought the intimate scene to a close. Max stood up, raising Barbara with him. 'You have a natural grace, Barbara. I think you will act your part admirably,' he smiled.

Their driver drove swiftly, slowing down only to pass through small towns and villages. Gerard had taken them only as far as the first town, where they had transferred to a hired carriage. Barbara was as anxious as Max to reach the coast, though Max tried to reassure her.

'We are English citizens on our way home,' he said lightly, in response to her anxious enquiry. He laid his hand reassuringly on hers. 'England isn't at war with France, though many would wish it! However, he is an unscrupulous adversary and I wouldn't put anything beyond him. Lesabre by name, Lescarabé by nature!'

Barbara frowned. 'Why do you say his name a little differently sometimes? Does it mean something in French?'

'Ha! Indeed it does!' Max laughed. 'A 'sabre' is a type of sword — a 'scarabe' is a beetle!' He grinned impishly. 'He does not like me to call him Monsieur le beetle!'

Barbara joined in his smile, forgetting their peril for a moment.

It was early evening when they entered the small seaport of Boulogne, later than Max had wanted. The tangy scent of the sea air was wafted inland on the fresh breeze. The inn Max chose faced the port. A ship was at anchor. They could see its masts silhouetted against the darkening sky.

After reserving their room and depositing their boxes, Max said he would go to book their passage on the first available vessel sailing to England. He hesitated as he turned to leave.

'You will be all right while I am gone?' he asked softly.

Barbara felt a rush of panic. She had been through so much in the past few days and only the presence of this man gave her the courage to see it through to the end.

'Yes . . . but I . . . '

Without intending it, her hand reached towards him, her unspoken need of his presence evident in the simple gesture.

Max smiled understandingly. He moved towards her and took hold of her hand, intending only to reassure her that he wouldn't be long.

Barbara looked up as if intending to speak but Max was lowering his head towards her. His slightly parted lips covered her mouth, moving softly, delighting in the sweet softness of her lips and the gentle acquiescence of her body to his demands.

With a small cry of distress, she pulled away. They stared at each other, the shock on Barbara's face mirrored by Max. She wanted to tear her glance away but she felt that the room was spinning around and she would fall if his steady gaze didn't hold her.

Max was the first to speak. 'Forgive me, Barbara. I didn't mean . . . ' He stopped. He had meant it. He had wanted to continue. He still did . . . but he felt like an inexperienced youth overcome by his first encounter with a maid. His heart thudded within his chest, its pulse gradually slowing as he regained control of himself. This wasn't the time or the place . . . and it wasn't the way he intended to proceed.

His hands fell to his sides and he

stepped away. 'I must go to book our passage. I won't be long.' He paused again in the doorway, not wanting to depart, yet knowing he must. 'I'll ask for a fire to be lit on my way out. It promises to be a cold night.'

The tiny window overlooked the sea. She gazed out, letting her imagination take her beyond the horizon. Was Catrine looking this way, longing for her love's return? How long was it since they had seen each other? Barbara had lost track of days. It must be at least a week. So much had happened, it seemed much longer.

A gentle knock at the door sounded, cutting short her silent thoughts and misgivings.

'Come in!' she called lightly, adding, 'Entrez!' in recollection of Catrine's response to her morning call.

It was the young serving girl who had shown them upstairs. She seemed very shy or nervous. 'Please, madame. I make the fire?'

'Yes, thank you!' She smiled at the

young girl, hoping to put her more at ease. It must be awkward for one so young to cope with a foreign language.

The fire soon warmed the small room, sending shadows dancing on the walls. By the time Barbara was feeling warmed through, Max returned. His manner was brisk as he removed his topcoat and strode over to the fire to warm his hands.

'The ship at the quayside is bound for England. It sails at ten o'clock in the morning on the high tide. However, the Captain wasn't aboard. Nor were any officers. I have to return in the morning to confirm our passage.'

Barbara was glad that he made no reference to their embrace. It was best to forget it had happened.

Lord Rockfort, as she must soon get used to calling him again, had obviously already done so.

He held out the crook of his arm to her. 'Come, Barbara. Our meal is ready downstairs. Remember to speak only English!' He made a lop-sided smile. 'In the eyes of this part of the world we are Lord and Lady Rockfort on our honeymoon in France.'

Barbara quenched the small feeling of sadness his allusion to their masquerade caused. Of course, that was the reason for his kiss! It was part of his charade . . . his attention to detail.

They ate a quiet meal seated by a huge open fireplace in the public room downstairs. Barbara was truly tired and thankful when Max escorted her back to their room.

'I will go downstairs again for half an hour. When I return, I will settle myself in that chair over there.' He kissed her lightly on the forehead. 'By tomorrow evening, we shall be home in England . . . and then we can resume our real lives.'

The daylight was streaming through the window when Barbara first opened her eyes. She sat up and looked across the room to the empty chair. Max must have awakened early and had probably gone to confirm their passage on the ship bound for England.

The air was chilled. The ashes from last night's fire were still in the grate. She shivered as she leapt out of bed. She splashed some water on her face and body and dressed swiftly, donning even her cloak to regain some heat. She was hungry. What were they to do about breakfast?

A quiet knock at the door heralded the maid. 'Please, madame! You come downstairs!' She pointed to the empty grate. 'Pas de feu, ici! No fire!' She smiled disarmingly. 'Big fire downstairs. Yes?'

Max had told her to stay upstairs during his absence last evening but surely he would think her a complete fool if she stayed up here in the chilly room when, downstairs, there was a roaring fire in the main public room. Anyway, he would be back soon and she would look out for him and call him over.

'Yes, that's kind of you,' she replied. She bent down before the looking-glass, hardly recognising her reflection. By this evening she would be Lady Rockfort no longer. She would enjoy this final day . . . and would have the memory of these few days of pretence for the rest of her life!

There were only two men in the public room. They were seated near the fire. As she hesitated, reluctant to approach too near to them, they both picked up their tankards and drained the last drops from them.

'Bonjour, citoyenne,' one murmured as they passed by. The other merely nodded.

'Bonjour, messieurs,' she replied automatically, inclining her head gracefully as she had seen Catrine do on numerous occasions.

'I bring you croissants, madame?' the maid asked timidly.

'Yes, please.' She seated herself at a small table near the fire.

'Alors, Mademoiselle Azaire! Vous nous rencontrons!'

The harsh voice startled her although

she didn't understand the words. She had been unaware of anyone's approach. She lifted her head ... and found herself face-to-face with Monsieur Lesabre.

For a moment, she was dumbfounded. Panic rose within her. Where was Max?

She looked around the room quickly ... but no-one else was there. Through her inner panic, Max's words came back to her. 'Speak only English! We are Lord and Lady Rockfort on our honeymoon in France.'

She raised her head imperiously. 'I beg your pardon, monsieur! I'm afraid I do not understand your words.'

'The serving maid tells me otherwise!' Lesabre said, in silky tones. 'You are a traitor, Citizen Azaire! You are wanted in Paris to answer for your treason against the State!'

Barbara recognised Catrine's name in the midst of the swiftly spoken words. Her hand flew to cover her throat, her bejewelled finger catching the light of a dancing flame from the fire.

'You . . . you are mistaken, sir!'

She tried unsuccessfully to control the quaver in her voice. 'I am Lady Rockfort, lately come from England. My . . . ' She couldn't help pausing. The word was still strange to her, ' . . . my husband and I are due to return there on the next crossing.'

Lesabre was nonplussed for a moment, suddenly uncertain of his victim's identity. He narrowed his eyes, indecision flickering across his face.

Barbara didn't know how well he knew Catrine. With her chestnut wig and fine clothes, she held a passing resemblance. She considered whipping off her wig to reveal her short curls but before she could do so, Lesabre's fist had struck the table in front of her.

'I don't care what you call yourself!' he hissed. 'You are an enemy of the new Republique and will meet the same fate as other such traitors!'

Barbara shivered at the venom in his

voice, her heart trembling. At the extreme edge of her vision she had spied movement. The two men who had earlier left the room had quietly returned . . . but so had Max. She forced herself to hold Lesabre's gaze.

Lesabre gestured to the two men to his right, rattling some words in French that Barbara sensed meant they were to take her outside. She held her breath.

'La, Lescarabé! I see you've met my wife!' Max said gaily, standing only a foot or so behind the man.

Lesabre spun round, his face twisted in fury. 'My name is Lesabre!' he corrected through tight lips.

Barbara almost laughed at the expression on his face. Almost . . . but not quite. She was still too apprehensive of what might happen.

Max took out his lorgnette and eyed Lesabre balefully through it. 'That's right! Lescarabé! Egad man! You don't look too well to me, sir! I would recommend a sea voyage to you — but not with us, alas! We have taken the last two berths on the next boat to England.' He bowed with a flourish of his hand, undisguised mockery in his deep eyes.

Lesabre straightened, backing away from the mocking figure who towered above him. He fumbled in an inner pocket of his long black coat. 'I have an order of arrest for this woman!' he floundered. 'It is written here! See!' He thrust the paper toward Lord Rockfort, who glanced at it carelessly.

Max shrugged slightly. 'My lady-wife is not the person you are persecuting!' he said dismissively. 'I know the lady in question . . . and she is soon to marry an English gentleman. She will be out of your jurisdiction, I'm pleased to say!'

'Soon — but not yet!'

'Before you can get at her!' He pulled out his fob-watch and glanced at it carefully. 'In eight hours time, I believe it to be!'

'Her marriage carries no weight in France!' Lesabre glared at him, full of hatred.

Max laughed lightly, returning to his dandified characterisation of a pleasure-seeking English lord, raising his lorgnette once more. 'Egad, sir! If you so much as lay one finger upon the lady in question, I assure you I will find you, whichever sewer you seek to hide in . . . and you will never come out of it alive!'

The words were said so calmly and quietly that Lesabre looked at him uncertainly, clearly wondering if he had misinterpreted their meaning.

Barbara hadn't! Her throat had tightened as Max spoke the hour of his wedding. So soon? She had hoped for some time. Time to become used to the idea. Not that she ever would become used to it, she admitted to herself! How would she bear it?

Max was still smiling . . . but his eyes were cold. He bowed stiffly. 'I bid you au revoir, monsieur!' He turned to Barbara. 'Come, m'dear. The air is suddenly quite putrid in here.' He gallantly held her hand in courtly fashion and the couple swept from the public room to a smaller, private room.

'You gave me a fright there, Barbara!' Max said lightly, in mock reproof. 'But I think you had the measure of him!'

Barbara's heart was numb. Had she heard correctly? He was to marry Catrine in eight hours time? 'We had better hurry aboard the ship, m'lord,' she said woodenly.

It was but a few yards to the landing stage. A sailor was waiting at the top of the gangway, bidding them hasten. Lifting the hem of her gown, Barbara hurried along at Max's side. No sooner had they stepped down into the boat than the sailor pulled in the gangway and a series of orders were shouted out in foreign tongue.

In spite of her confusion, Barbara felt excitement as the ship came alive beneath her. Her glance was drawn upwards as the sails billowed out, thrilled to see their magnificence unfold. She gasped at their beauty, marvelling at the power she could feel surge through the ship as it was gathered by the unseen hand.

Max had his arm about her waist and he led her towards the bows of the ship, where he paused by the rail, pointing forwards. 'Look! See how it cuts through the waves!'

Barbara looked. The bow of the ship seemed to slice through the waves like a knife, dipping and rising as it went. The wind whipped into her face, reminding her that she was still wearing the brown wig. Angrily, she leapt away from Max, wrenching the wig from her head.

'I don't need this any more!' she snapped. 'Our masquerade is no longer necessary, in case you hadn't noticed!'

He took hold of her hand, pulling her to him, his eyes sparkling with merriment. 'I have noticed that there is no-one to witness our kisses!'

Before she had time to protest, his mouth covered hers.

'No!' she finally managed a protest.

'I love you, Barbara!'

'What?' Her ears heard the words but her mind couldn't comprehend them.

'I love you!' he repeated.

Her heart stilled itself. 'You say that when you are to marry Catrine in . . . eight hours, was it?' Her tone was scathing.

'What?'

'Your wedding! In eight hours, in case you have forgotten!'

He laughed, his white teeth gleaming in the sunshine. 'I lied!' he said blithely.

'You lied?' Hope arose in her breast, even though she knew it was false.

'Yes. The wedding is tomorrow!'

'Oh!' Her cry of distress tore from her throat as she backed away from him.

'Barbara!'

'No! Don't touch me! I hate you!' She pulled the two rings off her finger and blindly held them out to him. 'Take these! Yes, both of them! They can never be mine! And I don't want to speak to you ever again!'

She whirled away, somehow finding

the steps down to the level below deck.

The only trouble was she didn't hate him! She loved him! And she really couldn't bear to imagine him with Catrine in his arms.

10

Barbara stayed below deck throughout the voyage, dreading the moment she would have to face Max again. Dreading even more the moment when she would come face to face with Catrine! How could she face her with love for Max in her heart? What could she say to her.

She suddenly knew that she could no longer be Catrine's maid. She loved her mistress and had thought to serve her after her marriage . . . but she now knew she couldn't! It would be impossible!

Maybe Lady Birchley would take pity on her and seek some other employment for her? Catrine would no longer be part of her household. Maybe she could stay there . . . in some other capacity? Anything would be preferable to having to witness Catrine's joy in her husband . . . and Max's joy in his wife — for, in spite of his words of love for her . . . she nearly choked on the memory . . . she knew it was but a momentary passion that had made him say them. How could it be otherwise?

It was late when they came in sight of land. The wind that had blown them so swiftly from the French coast had turned traitor and seemed determined to blow them back again. And Folkestone was farther from London than Dover.

'We must stay overnight,' Max informed her.

'Must we?' Barbara said coldly.

He seemed disturbingly unperturbed by her antipathy. 'Yes. I shall book us in at the 'Rose and Crown'. I have stayed there before and it is a reputable place.'

'You aren't afraid to lose your reputation yet further, then?' Barbara said icily.

'I will book separate rooms . . . at opposite ends of the tavern,' Max replied smoothly. 'Have no fear, Barbara! Your name shall not be sullied in England!'

She managed to maintain a haughty silence during their short carriage ride from the port to the tavern by determinedly keeping her face averted and once in the tavern she swept ahead of him to the room he reserved for her. Safe in her room, her composure fell and she sobbed out her grief, lying face-down on the narrow bed.

She was surprised to awaken in daylight, having tossed and turned for what seemed to be hours the previous night.

Today was the last day of her companionship with Lord Rockfort.

There was a knock at the door and a serving maid came into the room. 'Lord Rockfort asked me to assist you to dress, m'lady. He says your gown is in here.' She held out a large package and a round hat-box.

Barbara thought of dropping them on to the floor and stamping on them but knew that if he had bought her something new, it was only so that she would look decently dressed at Catrine's wedding.

She unwrapped the package and let the contents spill out on to the bed. The maid's gasp of delight echoed her inner reaction. It was beautiful!

Made of rich sapphire-blue silk, overlaid with a sprigged gossamer-light muslin, it was fashioned in the latest style. The sleeves were fitted, ending in a frill just above her elbows; a shoulder scarf of matching silk was held in place with a knot of tiny blue flowers and a wide sash covered the join in between the gathered bodice and the softly pleated skirt. Its colour reminded her of the ring Max had loaned her and she absently touched her finger where the ring had lain.

A small high-crowned hat with a narrow brim was rimmed with feathers and ribbons and would, in some measure, disguise her short-cropped curls. A pair of blue satin slippers lay in the bottom of the packet.

Barbara wanted to refuse the gift

. . . but it was for Catrine's wedding and she didn't want to disgrace her young mistress on such an important day.

With the maid's hasty administrations, she was quickly washed and dressed. The gown and slippers were exactly her size and a quick peek in the mirror revealed that she looked wonderful. She sighed gently. It would be difficult to go back to being a maid again, though she knew she must.

Max was already outside, speaking to their coachman. He looked very debonair in a dark crimson coat with wide, pointed revers and double row of golden buttons.

She nodded curtly in his direction. She couldn't speak for fear of bursting into tears, so she assumed a haughty expression as she took hold of his hand as he assisted her into the hired carriage.

Once their boxes were loaded Max climbed in beside her, giving the command to depart as he did so. He seated himself next to her, smiling in amusement as she inched herself away from him.

'You look beautiful,' he told her, his eyes showing the sincerity of his words.

She struggled to make her voice sound natural and cool. 'Thank you.'

Barbara's voice was no more than a whisper. 'Do you think this is a good idea? That I come to your wedding, I mean?'

He laughed, his right eyebrow rising. 'There is no-one I want more to be at my wedding, Barbara! But I . . . ' He reached out his hand to touch her.

Barbara leapt away, pressing herself against the side of the carriage. 'Don't touch me!'

Max made an impatient sound. 'If you say so!' His eyes narrowed, though if she had looked, she would have seen a strange glint in them. 'I was merely going to say that Catrine would be disappointed if you don't attend the marriage ceremony!'

She knew that was so.

It seemed an interminable journey. Barbara felt utterly wretched and each mile, each minute drew them closer to the time when he would be out of her reach forever.

Then, suddenly, they were there!

The carriage was halted. She heard Alfie's excited voice . . . and smiled, in spite of her misery. Max had leapt down from his outer seat and was opening the door for her. A number of people milled around, exclaiming at their lateness. Barbara glanced past them to where Alfie was holding the horses' bridle and smiled her delight at him. He grinned happily and put up his thumb.

'Good on yer, Miss Barbara!'

They were being hurried through the church gateway and along the path at the church door . . . and suddenly Lady Birchley appeared and enveloped Barbara in her arms, exclaiming her gratitude and wonder and delight.

They both laughed and cried at the same time, both exclaiming that it wouldn't do! It would spoil their faces. Yet still laughing and crying.

Lady Birchley disengaged herself and repeated the process with Max, eventually patting his back as if he were an infant in need of comfort. 'Go into the church, Max. Philip is waiting for you. He has the rings for you. Come with me, Barbara! Catrine is anxious to see you!'

With a cry of happiness, Catrine flung herself into Barbara's arms, caring nothing for the exquisite gown she was wearing. She looked radiant. If ever Barbara had hoped that she was only marrying Max because it was for her safety, the vibrancy of her face dispelled the notion.

'Barbara! Barbara! At last! I was so afraid for you! How can I ever thank you? You saved my life! I will love you for ever!'

Barbara laughed shakily. 'Max . . . Lord Rockfort would have saved you again . . . as he saved me!'

Catrine lifted her face, her eyes

clouded by a sudden sadness. 'No, Barbara. I would have killed myself long before then,' she said flatly.

Lady Birchley bustled forward. 'Now, girls! Wipe your eyes! We can't have the bride and bridesmaid crying, can we?'

'Bridesmaid?' Barbara echoed, her face blanching at the thought! No! She wanted to hide at the back where no-one could see her.

Catrine lifted her beautifully-long eyelashes and held out her hands. 'I want you to walk with me, Barbara. I want everyone to see my beautiful, brave friend! You will do this for me, yes?'

'Of course, she will, Catrine! Remove your hat, Barbara, so that I may fasten these flowers into your hair,' Lady Birchley commanded, holding out a blue and white floral coronet! 'Hurry now! The bridal march is about to begin!'

Barbara's hands lifted automatically to pull out the pins that held her hat in place. As she lifted the hat from her head, she heard both Catrine and Lady Birchley gasp.

'Your hair, Barbara!' Catrine gasped.

Barbara laughed shakily. 'I escaped dressed as a boy! I will tell you about it later!'

Catrine's eyes threatened to overflow once more. 'Your beautiful hair! You did it for me! Barbara, in my eyes, your hair is beautiful!' She hugged her again.

Barbara didn't remember setting off down the aisle behind Catrine, whose hand was resting lightly on the arm of a stately-looking man whom Barbara hadn't seen before. She only vaguely knew that they were approaching the figure of the minister . . . and, just to the right-hand side of him, were Max and Philip.

Both the men had turned to watch the bridal party approach. Barbara felt she couldn't bear to see Max's eyes as he beheld his bride but her eyes were drawn to his face of their own volition.

He was looking straight at her, his eyes warm with love.

The tiny laughter lines at the outer corners of his eyes were deeply etched. His mouth was curved into a smile. Barbara felt a moment of panic. What was he doing, smiling at her? He should be looking at Catrine! What would everyone be thinking?

She tried to shake her head at him . . . but he continued to smile at her. Was he mocking her? It wasn't like him to be so ungallant . . . but what other explanation was there?

Catrine had reached the front and turned round to hand her bouquet to Barbara. She took it blindly. Everything seemed to be in slow motion. The two men turned back to face the front as the minister began to intone the words of the marriage ceremony. Why was Philip standing next to Catrine? Why was the priest looking at him? She couldn't concentrate. She just wanted it to be over . . . then she could make her excuses and leave and find somewhere quiet where she could be alone.

'Do you, Philip Arthur George

Grafton, take this woman, Catrine Isobel Azaire, to be your lawfully wedding wife, to . . . '

The voice droned on . . . as Barbara's mind tried to sort out what she had heard. Philip Arthur George Grafton! He was marrying the wrong couple! Why did no-one stop him? Her head shot up, her lips opening to speak . . . but Max was looking over his shoulder at her, smiling idiotically at her, it seemed. His eyes seemed to be conveying a message, burning deeply into her own. What . . . ?

It hit like a bolt of lightning that was both illuminating and shocking at the same time! Catrine wasn't marrying Max! She was marrying Philip! How could she have been so stupid! As her face began to reflect her dawning knowledge, the expression on Max's face underwent a subtle change. His eyebrows rose a fraction and a laughing, teasing expression was sending a challenge to her.

She was suddenly confused. If Max

wasn't marrying Catrine, why had he said . . . ? Just what had he said? She suddenly wasn't sure. He had said he loved her . . . but that was for their charade, wasn't it? And he had let her think he was marrying Catrine!

Suddenly, she was angry with him — and she was totally unaware of the rest of the service. She walked back down the aisle with her hand on his arm, oblivious to the retreating figures of Philip and Catrine . . . to the congregation . . . to everyone except this insufferable man at her side. The man she loved! The man who thought fit to mock her!

Max patted her hand. 'Are we now back on speaking terms, my love?' he whispered in her ear.

Barbara tilted her nose into the air and turned her head away. 'No!'

'I love you, Barbara!'

'No you don't! It was all pretence, remember? You made sport of me!' She was being unfair, she knew. The charade had been necessary for her safety . . . but he could have ended it sooner.

Max grinned disarmingly. 'I want to make an honest woman of you!' he whispered.

She stopped abruptly and faced him, her face flushed. 'You are speaking foolishness! You cannot marry me! You would be ruined!'

Max gripped her arm just above her elbow and propelled her forward, down the aisle, almost to the door — but, at the last moment, he turned to the left and hustled her along the rear of the church into an ante-room.

She felt humiliated. 'How dare you! Have you no regard for propriety?'

'Apparently not!' he said coolly. 'What is the matter with you? I want to marry you, for heaven's sake!'

'There is no need, I assure you! No-one here knows what happened . . . and I am a nobody! It's not worth it — just for a bit of misplaced gallantry! I want you to leave me alone!' She stepped away from him, her head held high, willing herself not to weaken. Maybe he did think he loved her! It was only the excitement of the last few days!

'I don't love you!' she lied.

For a moment, he stared down at her, his face inscrutable. Then he abruptly turned on his heels and strode out of the room and, as far as she knew, out of her life!

Barbara stood, frozen to the space where she stood. He had gone! Had she hoped he would stay? She wasn't sure. She only knew she didn't want him to marry her out of pity.

It was only a short drive to Lady Birchley's home. The wedding breakfast was being held there and the servants were rushing around in a flurry of activity, taking cloaks and wraps off the guests and serving glasses of champagne from a never-ending supply, it seemed.

Barbara hardly knew any of the society people. Some she knew by sight, but none to speak to, reinforcing her opinion that Max would have regretted his offer of marriage. He was nowhere to be seen, for which she was thankful.

Lady Birchley wrapped her arms around her. 'Barbara! It has been selfish of us to rush you straight to Catrine and Philip's wedding — but the dear child wanted you to be there . . . and Max will have explained to you the need for her swift marriage to a man of some standing. Thank the Lord, Philip had already offered for her and that they are besotted with each other! Max is going to escort them to his home in Cornwall . . . but that is not until tomorrow. Now, Barbara, I have something important to tell you . . . but I am afraid it must wait. I must return to our guests. Run upstairs and I will send one of the servants to attend to you.'

Barbara was thankful when she was eventually left alone in the darkness of her room. Her emotions were in shreds and she no longer knew exactly what she had said to Max or, indeed, why. She laid a cool cloth over her forehead and eventually fell asleep.

She was awakened by Lizzie bringing in her breakfast on a tray. Lizzie pushed aside her protests. 'It's a pleasure, Miss Barbara! We're all that excited by what you did! You'll come and tell us all about it, won't you?'

'Eventually, Lizzie. It's a bit too fresh in my mind at the moment. I want to just forget it for now.' And forget Max and his smile . . . 'And I must get up and see Catrine, Mistress Grafton, I mean, before she leaves for Cornwall.'

'Oh, you're too late, Miss Barbara! They've gone! They left over an hour ago.'

Barbara's heart sank. It was too late to speak to Max. Philip and Catrine were to be his guests for a month . . . though how long Max would stay away was anybody's guess. Maybe he would stay away forever?

It was with a heavy heart that she rose and washed and dressed herself, putting on a gown that Lizzie brought for her to wear.

Lady Birchley met her in the

doorway of her room. 'Come in, dear. You're looking a bit better today, Barbara. I'm glad. I was unsure when to spring my surprise on you . . . but I think that right now could be the best time! There is someone I want you to meet!'

As they entered the lounge, a movement by the window caught her eyes. The figure turned towards them and slowly approached.

'I want you to meet Lord Randall, Barbara.' Lady Birchley paused, as if unsure how to proceed . . . then drew in her breath. 'He has something to tell you, dear.'

She turned to look at the man. He was a man of middle years and was smiling at her in a most endearing way.

'I knew your father, my dear. The Reverend Thomas Chesney. He helped me at a difficult time in my life.' He spread his hands. 'I had had an unfortunate disagreement with my father and was living in rough circumstances. I won't go into all of that now, it would serve no purpose. Suffice to say, your parents took me into their home and, after caring for me and restoring me to health and sanity, they arranged a meeting with my father and we were reconciled. I tried to contact him a few weeks later but a fever was raging in the city and anyone who could get out of the city had done so. Later, when the air was clear, I tried again to contact him but was told that he and his lady wife had died, leaving an orphaned daughter . . . but you had gone without trace.'

'Then I am pleased to meet with you, sir. I will be delighted to talk with you and hear more about my parents. I was but 3 years old when both of them died. But how have you now found me?'

'It was after you told Max about your father, Barbara,' Lady Birchley began to explain. 'Your name struck a memory chord but he couldn't think why. He began to make enquiries and was awaiting a reply when you were suddenly whisked from our midst.'

Barbara felt nonplussed. What was it leading to?

'My father set up a trust fund for you, hoping to find you,' Lord Randall continued. 'But, that was not to be. You had quite vanished . . . until, that is, Lord Rockfort began to make enquiries on your behalf. We have checked the dates of your birth and corroborated the story with your uncle. You are quite a wealthy woman, my dear!'

Lord Randall held out both his hands to Barbara. 'My father is now quite elderly and would dearly love to see you. I am here to invite you to visit us . . . to even take up residence with us, if that is your wish. I have never married. I intend to make you my heir. What do you say, my dear?'

'I think Barbara might have something else on her mind, right now, Lord Randall,' Lady Birchley murmured. 'You remember I introduced you to Lord Rockfort last evening?'

'Hmph! Yes! Young adventurer!'

'He saved Barbara's life . . . and remember what I said?'

'Hmph! About to make an offer, is he? What have you to say, my dear? Care for the fellow, do you?'

'I . . . ' Barbara was nonplussed. She recalled her harsh words to him, her refusal to listen to his declaration of love, her pride that had caused her to reject his proposal. And now . . . ? 'I fear it's too late!'

'It isn't too late, Barbara!'

The words were spoken quietly behind her. They sounded like music in her ears. She whirled round.

Max stood there, resplendent in tight cream breeches and dark green driving cape. 'I came back, Barbara. Prepared, if necessary, to copy Lesabre and abduct you!' He held out his hands. 'My words of love to you were true. They were not part of our charade. I fell in love with you before that . . . but could see no way to court you properly. I came to rescue you because I could not bear to live without you.' He suddenly looked uncertain.

She caught her breath. 'I . . . I love you, my Lord!'

'I know!'

Insufferable man!

'I still have two rings here!' Max patted his pocket.

Her heart leapt. 'My ring?'

He nodded solemnly. 'Your ring.' He reached into his pocket and pulled out the small velvet pouch, this time extracting only the sapphire ring. 'Barbara, will you marry me?'

Barbara dropped into a low curtsey. 'I shall be honoured to do so, my Lord.'

Max once more reached out for her left hand and selected her third finger. 'Then with this ring I pledge my troth!'

Lord Randall looked at Max from under his bushy eyebrows. 'Hmph! I expect you want to take her away from us as soon as we have gained her?' he demanded.

Max was unabashed. 'If I may, sir! I, too, nearly lost her!' He turned back to Barbara. 'If you agree, we are to accompany Philip and Catrine to my home in Cornwall. It is large enough for our two newlyweds to have whatever privacy they wish ... and for us to spend time together properly chaperoned by my household staff. Can you be ready within the hour?'

'Indeed she can!' Lady Birchley agreed. 'Take Lizzie as your maid, Barbara. Lord Rockfort will see to all proprieties, I know! And go shopping with Catrine when you get there. You will need a complete wardrobe!'

Max drew Barbara close to him, his lips looking very desirable, Barbara thought. 'Come, my love. We have a long journey ahead of us.'

Her French masquerade was over.

THE END

We do hope that you have enjoyed reading this large print book.

Did you know that all of our titles are available for purchase?

We publish a wide range of high quality large print books including:
Romances, Mysteries, Classics
General Fiction
Non Fiction and Westerns

Special interest titles available in large print are:
The Little Oxford Dictionary
Music Book, Song Book
Hymn Book, Service Book

Also available from us courtesy of Oxford University Press:
Young Readers' Dictionary
(large print edition)
Young Readers' Thesaurus
(large print edition)

For further information or a free brochure, please contact us at:
Ulverscroft Large Print Books Ltd.,
The Green, Bradgate Road, Anstey,
Leicester, LE7 7FU, England.
Tel: (00 44) **0116 236 4325**
Fax: (00 44) **0116 234 0205**

CONVALESCENT HEART

Lynne Collins

They called Romily the Snow Queen, but once she had been all fire and passion, kindled into loving by a man's kiss and sure it would last a lifetime. She still believed it would, for her. It had lasted only a few months for the man who had stormed into her heart. After Greg, how could she trust any man again? So was it likely that surgeon Jake Conway could pierce the icy armour that the lovely ward sister had wrapped about her emotions?

TOO MANY LOVES

Juliet Gray

Justin Caldwell, a famous personality of stage and screen, was blessed with good looks and charm that few women could resist. Stacy was a newcomer to England and she was not impressed by the handsome stranger; she thought him arrogant, ill-mannered and detestable. By the time that Justin desired to begin again on a new footing it was much too late to redeem himself in her eyes, for there had been too many loves in his life.

MYSTERY AT MELBECK

Gillian Kaye

Meg Bowering goes to Melbeck House in the Yorkshire Dales to nurse the rich, elderly Mrs Peacock. She likes her patient and is immediately attracted to Mrs Peacock's nephew and heir, Geoffrey, who farms nearby. But Geoffrey is a gambling man and Meg could never have foreseen the dreadful chain of events which follow. Throughout her ordeal, she is helped by the local vicar, Andrew Sheratt, and she soon discovers where her heart really lies.

HEART UNDER SIEGE

Joy St Clair

Gemma had no interest in men — which was how she had acquired the job of companion/secretary to Mrs Prescott in Kentucky. The old lady had stipulated that she wanted someone who would not want to rush off and get married. But why was the infuriating Shade Lambert so sceptical about it? Gemma was determined to prove to him that she meant what she said about remaining single — but all she proved was that she was far from immune to his devastating attraction!

HOME IS WHERE THE HEART IS

Mavis Thomas

Venetia had loved her husband dearly. Now she and their small daughter were living alone in a beautiful, empty home. Seeking fresh horizons in a Northern seaside town, Venetia finds deep interest in work with a Day Centre for the Elderly — and two very different men. If ever she could rediscover love, would Terry bring it with his caring, healing laughter? Or would it be Jay, the once well-known singer now at the final crossroads of his troubled career?